W9-DDO-877

Too
Many
Promises

by RUTH FORBES CHANDLER

Illustrated by Ray Scott Campbell

ABELARD-SCHUMAN
New York

Printed and bound in the
United States of America

Published simultaneously in Canada
by Nelson, Foster & Scott Ltd., Toronto

To Charles and Frances

CONTENTS

Chapter 1 **GOODBYE TO OLD FRIENDS**

It was an hour to train time, but Niki Louganis was
ready to go. His grandmother and his mother had
said everything they had to say over and over, and
now the silence was harder to bear than the talking
had been.

Niki looked at the clock. Its loud ticking insisted
that it was marking time, but the hands seemed not
to move. Unable to sit still any longer, he removed
his long legs from the arm of the most comfortable
chair in the room and stood up.

"I may as well go along," he said.

As though the words were a signal, the women rose, too.

"I'll walk to the station with you," his mother said.

"What for?" Niki asked impatiently. He was fifteen, and didn't think he had to be walked to the station as if he were a little child.

He bent his head to give his grandmother a quick peck on her cheek. It seemed strange to be taller than she was, to be able to look down at her as she stopped him, putting her hands on his shoulders.

"Niki, sure and you're a fine lad," she said, her words tingling with pride, "a fine, handsome lad." Puckering his lips, Niki blew along the part in her thick white hair. She pushed him away, her eyes flashing. "And if you get into trouble again, may the divil take you."

Niki laughed. He and his grandmother understood each other. In some ways she was nearer to him than his mother was, for while she often lashed him loudly with her tongue, she did it as a duty, for the good of his soul, and having done it, felt better. But his mother's hurt went deeper. Since his father's death Niki was the center around which her life revolved, and he felt guilty and uncomfortable with her because he could not forget the desperate, heart-breaking worry he caused.

He saw it in her eyes as she said, "I'm going down to the door with you. Have you got everything?"

Yes, Niki had everything, including the lunch in a candy box that they had insisted he must take. But he also had in his wallet the ten dollars his mother had given him, a new suitcase for his clothes, his camera, everything he would need for the summer. His spirits rose as he carried his bag carefully down the narrow stairs.

In the lower hall he turned to face his mother.

"Let me say it this time," he said, pitching his voice high like a little child's. "I must be a good boy and work hard and not sound off every time I don't like something. I must keep away from bad company, because it's this or reform school, and I must justify Mr. Morgan's faith in me for it's my last chance."

He broke off suddenly, for his mother was crying.

"Mom, don't," he said, the mocking banter gone from his voice. "I mean it. I really do. I promise I'll try as hard as I can."

"So many promises! If I could only believe that this time you do mean it."

"I do," he interrupted. "Before the end of the summer I'll be running the farm, and I'll have both the Barnards and their rabbits eating out of my hand. Don't you believe it?" As he aimed a kiss at her eyebrow he saw that she was smiling through her tears. "'Bye now. I'll write to you tonight, and two or three times every week."

He got out as fast as he could and then blew a deep sigh. "Women!" he muttered, but, at the corner, he turned to wave to them as they watched from the window.

It was a fine June morning. He whistled happily as he walked the five blocks to the station. Everything had turned out fine. After all the weeks of worry, he was getting exactly what he had always wanted, a summer in the country. You couldn't call it a vacation, he thought, because he would have to work, but probably not much. He loved animals. It wouldn't be work to take care of them. And Mr. Morgan, the principal at Warren High, and Niki's good friend, had said that everybody liked the Barnards. Niki was sure he would like them, too.

And he would make them like him. He could do that to people when he tried. With the Barnards it would be easy. They were lonely. A month ago their youngest son had been killed in an explosion on an aircraft carrier where he was in training. His parents were heartbroken, of course. They had consented to take Niki for that reason, Mr. Morgan said. It wouldn't be quite so lonesome with a boy around.

At the station he bought his ticket and sat down

to wait forty more minutes. He liked being there, watching people come and go. Soon a boy in faded dungarees and a pink plaid shirt slid into the seat beside him.

"Hiya, Niki," he said.

"Hi, Jokey. What's up?"

"Mr. Morgan went to see the man in Greenfield. He's got a big service station and garage, and he'll take me. I go Thursday. I think I'll like it." He stretched his long legs across the aisle and shoved his hands deep into his pockets. "You know," he went on, " you and me, we're lucky."

"Don't I know it!" Niki agreed.

Until train time they sat there, not talking much, but thinking the same thoughts. They had been friends for years, attending the same schools, playing on the same teams, getting into small troubles as all boys do, but never anything serious until the winter day when they discovered Deego Silver working around the gas station at the corner of their street. From then on they had been in trouble, real trouble, most of the time.

Deego was nineteen. He represented all they wished for. He was through school; he had a job and money to spend; he had a car. Nobody could make him write reports or work out equations in algebra. Nobody cared where he went or how late he stayed

out at night. He boasted that nobody could tell him
what he could or could not do, not even the police.

Niki and Jokey, who would have howled like a
hurricane if they had to shake a mat over the rail for
their mothers, spent hours polishing Deego's car and
helping him with the jobs he had to do. Rides with
him and his friends were their reward. Deego drove
with a heavy hand on the horn and a heavy foot on
the gas, burning up the road on the super-highways,
wiggling in and out of city traffic, and parking in a
space five inches longer than his car, with one turn
of the wheel. Doing homework couldn't compete
against talent like that. Truancy on Deego's day off
became a habit. It made trouble, but it was worth it.

As the weeks passed and the difficulties at school
and at home increased, the two boys turned more and
more to Deego and his gang. They worked off their
resentment against parents and teachers by upsetting
ash barrels and smashing windows. One thing led to
another. They had occasional brushes with the police,
but Deego said, "Aw, forget it." So they did, for
Deego was their leader and what he said was good
enough for them. Deego was all right.

And then, one lovely moonlight night in May,
they found out differently. Deego was not all right.
He was afraid of cops. He was yellow, a dirty yellow
coward.

That night had begun like many others. Deego had packed seven of them into his car and taken them to a pavilion near a lake. They ate ice cream and played the pinball machines for a while, then came out to find a new Lincoln parked beside their car, its windows open, the keys in the ignition.

"Dare you, Deego," Pete, one of the older boys, said. "Take us down to the crossroads in that. What do you say?"

"Sure," he had answered. Before they got to the crossroads they heard a siren wailing behind them. Deego stepped on it —how that Lincoln could travel! Niki leaned over Deego's shoulder, yelling with excitement, as he watched the needle swing to fifty, sixty, seventy, seventy-five. Warnings of an intersection flew by, but nothing could stop them as they shot through the red lights, missing one car by inches and sending another off the road.

Suddenly, it wasn't fun any more. Niki pushed back into the seat beside Jokey, his heart hurting in his throat, his eyes squeezed shut, his fists clenched tight, waiting . . . . The end came fast, with squealing rubber and a skid that threw them to the floor as the car left the road on a curve, plowed across the soft ground, and crashed against a tree.

Niki still felt sick as he remembered. He might be dead now. It was a chilling thought, but no worse than remembering the other things—Dick Stevens jammed into the front seat by the broken door, and Pete . . . Niki couldn't bear to look. He had turned and staggered away on trembling legs as Jokey helped Deego take Pete out and lay him on the grass.

Then the police came. When Niki turned back, they were taking names and asking questions.

"You were driving," they said to Deego.

"No, I wasn't driving," he answered, his face white, his mouth working horribly. "Not me. Pete was driving." He pointed to the twisted form on the ground. "He was driving. Not me."

Niki leaned against a tree to steady himself, trembling with fury against Deego, sick again with nausea, frightened as he had never been before in all his life. They questioned him last. He answered as the others had done. Yes, Pete was driving. And then the ambulance came and took the injured boys to the hospital. They were still there. Deego and two others were awaiting sentence to jail or reform school. But because Niki and Jokey were only fifteen, and because Mr. Morgan had assumed responsibility for their good behavior, they were released in his custody. Niki echoed Jokey's words. Yes, they were lucky. In more ways than one.

When the train came, Niki was the first passenger aboard, on his way at last. As it speeded through

big cities and suburbs, out into the country with
occasional glimpses of rivers and hills, flower-filled
fields and dairy barns, Niki was filled with great excitement. But, when he opened the candy-box lunch,
he was suddenly homesick. He had never been away
from home, alone, before. When the boy came
through the train selling cold drinks and candy, Niki
ordered a coke, and giving him a quarter, told him
to keep the change. That made him feel better, and,
as he ate his chicken sandwiches and brownies, he
smiled and turned his thoughts towards Bristol and
the Barnards.

Chapter 2 INTRODUCING THE BARNARDS

So the boy was coming today.

Charles Barnard ran his fingers through his thick white hair and slumped lower on the divan, frowning at the letter in his hand.

Why, in Heaven's name, had he told Tom Morgan he would take this boy? He didn't want to be bothered with anybody around the place, especially this fellow. Unfolding the letter from the principal of the high school in Warren, where he himself had taught for many years, Charles Barnard read the closing paragraph again.

18

"Niki knows this is his last chance and that he will have to work," Morgan had written. "He should be a real help to you because he likes animals. He is quick and intelligent. I believe that in the new environment, with you to take an interest in him, he will turn out all right. And, Charlie, take this from an old friend. He will be good for you right now, too."

Charles Barnard's lips curled in a bitter smile. Sure. This young rascal who had been mixed up in a half dozen kinds of trouble was all he needed to make life perfect. He knew Niki's kind, a good enough boy who suddenly stops working and gets into trouble with his teachers. Then he becomes a truant, and the next step down the ladder is signing his parent's name to the slips sent home. When the attendance officer catches up with him, he finds himself in trouble both places, becomes defiant, joins up with a gang who are in similar difficulties, and goes from bad to worse.

Well, one thing was certain: the boy would work or he would go back to the city — fast. And another was even more certain: he would not be permitted to go into the chinchilla house even if he did "like animals." Too much money was tied up in that business to have an irresponsible young hellion meddling around. Lost in his thoughts, Charles Barnard sat there, staring at nothing.

His wife called from the doorway, "Isn't it nearly time to go to the station, Charles?" She paused a second and added, "To get our boy?"

He looked at her. White hair, pink cheeks, white dress, pink apron. Such a frail little bit of a woman, but she was braver than he was. She really wanted this boy to come.

"All right, Martha. Let's go."

They drove to the station in silence, their minds filled with memories and troubled thoughts. And now this new problem. What kind of boy would this stranger be who was to share their home for the summer?

The car parked, they walked through the station. As the train whistle shrieked, Mrs. Barnard slipped her hand into her husband's. His fingers closed over hers with reassuring pressure as the train pulled in.

There was the boy on the platform, tall, dark, slender, neatly dressed, his black eyes searching the crowd, then finding the Barnards. His face lighted in a broad smile. In an instant he was down the steps, hurrying towards them.

"You're Mr. and Mrs. Barnard." It was a statement, not a question. "I'm Niki. I knew you the minute I saw you," he added, as they shook hands.

"How did you recognize us so quickly?" Mrs. Barnard asked.

"Mr. Morgan told me to look for the tallest man at the station with lots of white hair, and a little bit of a woman with the sweetest face in the world."

"I can't imagine Tom Morgan ever saying that," said Mrs. Barnard.

"I found you, didn't I?" Niki persisted, with a wide smile that showed his even white teeth.

Charles Barnard was disappointed and angry. No boy could take the place of his son. He knew that. But did Tom Morgan have to choose this smooth, cocky, conceited young — he searched for a word — actor? That's what the boy was — master of the situation, Master of Ceremonies, as he appraised his host and hostess.

"All right. Come on. The car's over here," he said abruptly. "Get in back, Nikolas."

"Mr. Morgan sent his best wishes to you, sir. I suppose he told you why he asked you to take me."

"Yes. We know." The man and boy sized each other up for a minute in silence. Then Niki stepped into the car.

"Mr. Morgan's a swell guy. Some of the boys got sent away, but Jokey Perry and I got another chance because he promised to be responsible for our good behavior. I hoped you would take both of us."

Mr. Barnard stepped on the starter and made the engine roar.

"God forbid," he said softly.

"I've never lived in the country, so I don't know much about it, but I'll learn quickly. I've always wanted to milk a cow. Have you got one?" Niki leaned over the front seat eagerly.

Mr. Barnard was apparently absorbed in driving the car, so his wife answered. "Yes, we have two cows, about a hundred hens, and a large vegetable garden. That will keep you busy. And later on, when we get our irrigating system, Mr. Barnard is going to get out a small nursery — pine trees, and junipers. Would you like to help him plant a thousand little trees?"

"Sure," said Niki. "And, Mr. Barnard, I'll take care of your rabbits for you. I raised some rabbits once in my back yard, so I know all about them. Mine were just ordinary rabbits. Mr. Morgan says you raise chinchillas. Is that a special kind?"

Mrs. Barnard saw her husband's jaw tighten as it always did when he was annoyed. Before he could reply, she interrupted, "Look, Niki, there is our new high school. It cost half a million dollars, and it will be opened for the first time this fall. And there's the Town Hall and the Post Office. The stores are on this street we're crossing now. Bristol isn't a large village, but we think it's a pretty one."

The boy looked at the quiet, elm-shaded street,

the common, the village church with its tall white spire.

"Any movies?" he asked.

"Yes."

"How often do they change the pictures?"

"I'm not sure. We don't go very often, but it will tell in the paper."

Niki studied first one profile and then the other. Mr. Barnard's face was sunburned to a deep, healthy, copper color. It was a strong face, with a large, straight nose and square jaw. His lips were drawn tightly; his expression was grim. He may like boys, Niki thought, but he certainly doesn't like me . . . not yet. Mrs. Barnard's face was soft and pink, creased with tiny wrinkles that disappeared when she smiled. And she was trying to be nice.

But Niki was too excited to keep still long.

"Have you a television set?" he asked.

"No. We have a radio, but no television. Look! There's Indian Pond where all the boys go swimming. We're almost home now. See the little house on the top of the hill?"

They turned into a driveway and stopped at a gray-shingled cottage, half hidden by shrubs and climbing roses. Along one side a screened porch was furnished as an outdoor living room. Beyond the house were a large barn and several smaller buildings.

Looking to his left, across the lawn and beyond the flower gardens, Niki saw the pond sparkling in the sunshine, with fields, woods and hills stretching out to the horizon.

"Oh boy, what a place!" Niki cried. He was out of the car in an instant, running up the drive for a better view when a huge boxer bounded towards him.

"Down, Hercules," commanded Mr. Barnard.

"That's all right," said Niki, standing motionless. "I'm not afraid. I like dogs. He'll just smell around and find that out."

"He's trained to be a watch dog. He doesn't like strangers."

"You mean he's had obedience training? I've read about that and how dogs will heel and stay and do whatever they are told. It's wonderful what you can teach a dog. Some of them go to school and get diplomas." Slowly Niki dropped to one knee. "Did you get a diploma, boy? Did you get all A's? I'll bet you did. Come on, tell me about it."

The big dog sniffed the outstretched hand and went a little nearer.

"We're going to be friends, you know. Want me to rub your ears, boy, just a little, gently, like this?" Carefully Niki touched the big head, moving his fingers back and forth in slow rhythm at the base of the dog's ears, gently at first, then with deep, firm pressure, talking softly all the while. "You like that, don't you? Sure and you're smooth as velvet, and it's beautiful brown eyes you've got. From this day we're friends, Herky, and don't you be forgetting it."

"Niki, are you Irish? You talk as though you'd kissed the Blarney stone," said Mrs. Barnard.

"No. Not me. But my grandmother is. My Grandmother Przybyzewski."

"Niki, what are you saying!"

"It's the truth. She's Irish, but she married a Pole. So my mother is half Irish, half Polish. My father's mother was Italian. She married a Greek. His name was Nikolas Louganis. So was my father's. In me you see the United Nations." Niki thumped his chest and grinned.

Mr. Barnard turned away abruptly and stalked off.

"What's the matter with him?" Niki asked. "Did I say something I shouldn't?"

"It's all right," Mrs. Barnard told him. "Take your bag and I'll show you your room."

They entered the house through the kitchen, and passed through a pretty living room with bright curtains and comfortable well-worn chairs. Books and magazines were everywhere. Niki had never seen so many except at school, or in the Public Library.

Up steep narrow stairs they went to the bedroom.

Niki stopped on the threshold. It was a wonderful room, beyond all doubt a boy's room. The curtains were deep blue, the walls cool gray, the spread on the narrow bed had a design of ships woven into it. There were bookshelves, a bureau, a table. Two big wicker chairs with blue cushions stood beside the windows.

"Was this . . . was this Lewis's room, Mrs. Barnard?" Niki asked softly.

"No, we wouldn't put you in Lewis's room." Then she caught the look in the boy's eyes. "I'm ashamed of myself for saying that, Niki, but we haven't quite got used to having Lewis . . . gone."

"That's all right. It's a fine room. I never had a room of my own since we lived at my grandmother's. That's all I meant."

Mrs. Barnard was not listening. "Lewis was a fine boy," she went on, her eyes on the farthest hills. "Our youngest. Richard, our other son, was killed on Okinawa. When the word came about Lewis, it seemed as if it was more than we could bear."

"I know. Mr. Morgan told me. My father was lost on a destroyer in the Pacific. I was just a little kid then, but I know how you feel."

Her lips trembled for a minute, then she continued. "Wars are terrible things, Niki, but we have to go on living. That's why I persuaded Charles to take you. He has always liked boys."

"They liked him, too," Niki interrupted. "Mr. Morgan says he was the best math teacher they ever had, and that everybody was sorry when he resigned."

"He just isn't himself these days. You mustn't mind his moods. You made him think of Lewis when you were talking out there in the yard."

"I did?" asked Niki, surprised.

"Our son was named for his father and grand-father just as you were. He was the third Charles Lewis Barnard." She bit her lips and her eyes filled with tears.

"I'm awfully sorry." There was an awkward silence as she fought for self-control and Niki tried to think of something to say.

"You know," he said at last, "I think Mr. Barnard and I will get along fine together. I promised Mr. Morgan I wouldn't quit or get thrown out before the summer is over. And that's one promise I mean to keep. I'll help Mr. Barnard every way I can, especially with his rabbits."

She smiled through her tears and left him to unpack his bag.

Chapter 3   CHINCHILLAS ARE NOT RABBITS

Quickly Niki unpacked the shirts and slacks his mother had ironed and folded so carefully, and laid them in one of the big, empty bureau drawers. As he lifted his pajamas, he found beneath them a large flat package wrapped in white paper and tied with blue string. He turned it over in his hands with a twinge of conscience. His mother was so good to him! It was just like her to slip a surprise into his suitcase.

As he untied the string and opened the box, he thought of the candy bars he had found so often in his lunch box when he was a little kid. But it wasn't

28

a candy bar this time. It felt more like a picture, a small, framed picture. He unfolded the tissue paper that protected the glass and sat staring at what he had uncovered.

A face that might have been his own looked at him from the photograph. The same black hair, the same deep wave that all the girls envied, the same dark eyes, even white teeth, and broad smile. It was his father's graduation picture, his mother's way of saying what she could not put into words. He placed it on the bureau between the alarm clock and the pin tray, stood looking at it for a minute, then finished unpacking. That done, he dressed in his work clothes and went to the kitchen.

"What do you want me to do first?" he asked Mrs. Barnard.

"Aren't you hungry, Niki?"

"Well, yes, I am. I had a couple of sandwiches and a coke on the train, but that was a long time ago."

She set out a can of molasses cookies and a bottle of milk.

"My mother told me not to eat you out of house and home the first day," he said, "but to let it come gradually. I've got an awful appetite." He paused after six cookies and three glasses of milk.

She smiled at him. "Don't eat so much you can't

eat your supper. I want you to pick some peas for me, and down at the end of the garden you'll find the strawberries. We have dinner at noon and a light supper at night."

Niki did justice to that light supper, the big bowl of green peas swimming in rich milk with a golden haze of butter on top, light, hot biscuits and thin slices of ham, and strawberries and cream. He moved slowly with a pleasant sense of fullness as he got up from the table.

Mr. Barnard rose, too. "We'll get the cows now, Nikolas, and I'll show you how to milk. Let me see your hands." Niki spread them out, long, slender hands, lightly calloused from swinging a bat. "Hm," Mr. Barnard said, "you'll have to go easy on hoeing for a while or you'll have a fine crop of blisters."

"I've got a lot to learn, I know," Niki said as they walked down the lane to the pasture, "but I'm willing to do anything you tell me." He glanced up to see if that softened the stern face beside him. It did not.

"I expect you to help in the garden and do some of the barn chores," Mr. Barnard said. "And next week you can help with the haying. But your first duty is to do whatever Mrs. Barnard asks you to. She, well, she's been through a lot these past weeks, and I'm worried about her."

He paused, and Niki, sensing it was the right thing to do, said nothing.

"You'll have to do the scrubbing and any heavy lifting and everything else you can that will save her work. That is the only reason I said I would take you. She seemed to want me to."

"Yes, sir," Niki answered. "I understand. I'll help her."

They walked on in silence to the lower pasture where two sleek Jersey cows were waiting at the bars.

As soon as the gate was opened, they made their way along the lane and into the barn where each found her stall. Mr. Barnard gave them grain, washed his hands and the cows' udders, seated himself on a three-legged stool and milked. That seemed to be all there was to it, squeeze and pull, squeeze and pull. Niki watched carefully as the streams of milk squirted into the silver-bright pail. Tomorrow morning he would have his chance to try, and he could hardly wait.

That evening the sun set in a glow of pink and gold. The clouds caught the glory of it. It was reflected in softer tones in the quiet waters of the pond. As Niki sat on the grass watching the changing colors, he talked softly to Hercules, who was keeping his part of the friendship pact by trying to be a lap dog.

"I wish I could paint it or put it into words when I write to my mother tonight. She'd love this place. But it's so quiet, it kind of gets you, doesn't it, Herky?"

It wasn't that he was homesick, but somehow he couldn't stop thinking about his mother. Like the clouds, his thoughts lost their brightness as he remembered her in Mr. Morgan's office. It was as though he were there again, hearing her speak the words, and seeing her hands nervously clasping and unclasping the fastener on her handbag as she looked from him to Mr. Morgan.

"Please give him another chance," she was pleading. "I begged him not to go with those boys. I told him they were no good, but he wouldn't listen to me. If only his father were here to help me ... . I don't know what to do with him."

Mr. Morgan felt sorry for her, Niki could see that, as he read the list of offences committed by Deego and his gang. There was no longer any use in Niki's denying that he had taken part in many of them.

His mother bowed her head, speaking in a voice that was only a whisper. "The police came to our house about the broken windows and the damage to the school building, and of course I knew about the car. I didn't know that there were other things."

Niki couldn't look at her then. He still felt the tightness in his throat as he thought about it. He hadn't played fair with her, staying out until one or two o'clock in the morning and refusing to tell where he'd been. He wished he could forget the hateful things he had said to her because she waited up for him. And then, the awful mess about the stolen car. She had been right about Deego. And it was she to whom he really owed his thanks for his last chance.

He lifted his head and looked at the quiet land-scape, breathing the sweet scent of honeysuckle, listening to bird songs that came like questions and answers from the woods near by.

"I don't deserve it, Herky, but this time I will make good. I'll make it up to her for all the worrying. I swear I will."

As rubbed the dog's dark muzzle he watched the fading colors turn blue-gray, dark gray, with only a faint, pearly afterglow to show where the sun had set. It must be nearly nine. He must go in and write that letter.

As he walked towards the house, he met Mr. Barnard.

"Can I help you do something?" Niki asked.

"No. I'm just taking a last look at the chin-chillas."

"Oh, the rabbits," Niki said, looking up hopefully. He sure would love to see those chinchilla rabbits.

"Chinchillas are not rabbits," Mr. Barnard said coldly. "They cost me around fifteen hundred dollars a pair."

Niki's eyes popped. "Jeepers!" he exclaimed. "Could I look at them?"

"Well," Charles Barnard said, hesitating. He had a fine herd of chinchillas, and he was very proud of them. Showing them to people was always a pleasant task . . . and the boy would have to see them some time, he supposed.

"Well," he repeated, "all right. Come along."

Niki waited for him to fit the key into the Yale lock and open the door. Then they stepped into the chinchilla house. There, on shelves, ranged one above the other, were large wire cages and in them were the precious little animals.

No, they weren't rabbits. Niki could see that as soon as he looked at them. They were smaller than rabbits, more the size of large squirrels, with round ears and tiny forepaws. Their tails were shorter than squirrels' tails, not curled over their backs, not as bushy. But it was their fur that Niki noticed most of all, their long, thick, blue-gray fur. He wished he could touch it, for it looked as soft as down.

As he watched, some of them dashed around the

sides of their cages, others sat up, their tiny forepaws against their chests, looking at Niki wth shoe-button bright eyes.

"Gosh, where have I been all my life thinking chinchillas were rabbits?" he whispered softly, so as not to frighten them. "They eat hay?" Bits of it were lying about the floor, so it was not exactly a question.

Charles Barnard nodded, watching the boy go slowly and quietly from cage to cage. It was evident that he was fascinated, and he had sensed without being told that chinchillas would be disturbed by loud voices and abrupt movements. Maybe Tom Morgan was right after all. Niki was a clean, nice-looking boy, certainly intelligent, and trying hard to please. Even if he could put on a good act, his interest in the chinchillas was genuine.

Mr. Barnard smiled a lop-sided smile, not at Niki, but at himself, remembering that the chinchilla house was the one place he had vowed to keep the boy out of. Well, he couldn't hurt them any by looking.

"You've got forty of them," Niki said, after visiting all the cages.

"Forty-six," Mr. Barnard corrected. "Some are in the nesting boxes at the back."

Niki turned his attention to the nesting boxes which were attached to every cage, giving a dark hide-out for privacy. He looked again at the hollow logs where the little animals could play, and which they could gnaw on; he inspected the wire floors covered with dark brown chips, which Mr. Barnard explained were chopped sugar cane; he noticed there were sliding pans under the floors of the cages to make sanitation easy.

"Pretty slick," he said. "You're lucky to have all this and forty-six chinchillas."

"I've done pretty well. I started with three pairs when I retired four years ago."

"Wow! What an easy way to make money!" Niki exclaimed, trying to figure out what forty-six times one half of fifteen hundred dollars would come to.

"It's not as easy as it may sound to you," Charles Barnard said, unhooking the screen door and waiting for Niki to leave. "All right now, you've seen them. If you want to know more about them, you'll find magazines in the house published by different organizations of chinchilla breeders."

"I'm going to read them all," Niki said earnestly. "I'm going to learn all there is to learn about this business."

"That should keep you busy for one summer."

The rest of the evening passed quickly as Niki entered a new world of chinchilla lore. "Look at all the ribbons and prizes this one got," he said, showing a picture to Mr. Barnard. "Have any of yours ever won prizes?"

"No, but I have one that should get a ribbon this fall if I decide to enter him in a show."

"I should think yours would all be champions. They look just like the picture."

Niki heard the mellow tone of the grandfather clock in the hall and stopped to count it. Ten o'clock. He stood up and stretched. It had been a long day. "I suppose I ought to go upstairs now and write a letter to my mother. Believe you me, I've got a lot to tell her!"

After the goodnights were said, there was silence in the sitting room. Charles Barnard pretended to read a magazine, but his wife noticed he turned no pages. She sighed as she reached for her scissors to clip a new recipe for mincemeat cookies from the evening paper.

I'll make some tomorrow for Charles and Niki, she thought. If only I could feel sure that boy was genuine, and not just putting on an act to please us.

Chapter 4 **A LOT TO LEARN**

Those hot June days were the busiest Niki had ever
known. And how he ached! He discovered muscles
he never knew he had, but he knew now. Sometimes
he felt sore from head to foot; his hands were blis-
tered; his back sunburned. He was so deep in sleep
when the alarm went off at six-thirty that he could
hardly drag himself out of bed. But breakfast was
already cooking, and it smelled good. It was a working man's breakfast, and Niki needed it, for he was a
working man.

Learning to milk Brownie and Bess was the high-spot of the barn chores. He knew very little about cows, but Niki imitated Mr. Barnard's technique as exactly as he could. The results, however, were quite different, for as soon as he sat down beside Bess she turned inquiring eyes to see what had happened and switched her tail in his face to show her disapproval. At first no milk came, and when it did the sudden squirts went everywhere, except into the pail.

Niki was patient. He talked to her gently.

"All right, Bess. Hold still. I'm doing the best I can. If you'd just do your part it would help a lot." The sweat poured from his red face.

Every morning and night he kept at it, and by the end of the week he could milk. Although it took him much longer, he could strip Brownie and Bess as dry as Mr. Barnard could. That was something!

After pasturing the cows in the lower meadow, Niki had the hens to feed. He enjoyed the hens. They were the comedians of the farm. One, especially, reminded him of a high school teacher, a fussy, clucking big-bosomed woman who looked as though she were stuffed with feathers, and who had Rhode Island red hair.

"Come on, Lydia," Niki would say, grinning at the hen as she came hurrying up, cocking her head sideways, and looking at him with her round black eyes. "Oh, don't be so greedy. Give the other girls a chance."

It was the animals he liked. To him they were personalities. The other chores, like cleaning out stalls and fumigating the henhouses, were only jobs to get done. Cutting the grass and trimming hedges were all right, when his hands weren't sore, because the lawn looked like clipped green velvet when he finished and he could be proud of his work. The things he did in the house to help Mrs. Barnard were done willingly, too, for she reminded him a little of his grandmother, and he felt a kindly, protective feeling towards her because of Lewis.

And washing windows, polishing floors — anything was better than hoeing! The rows of corn and potatoes seemed endless. Weeding out the purslane and dog-grass from the onions and carrots was even slower work. Every fifteen minutes Niki would straighten his aching back and count the blisters and callouses on his hands.

"Gosh, farming is hard work," he would say. But Mr. Barnard was keeping steadily at it in another part of the field, so Niki would sigh and tackle his own row once more.

But the days were not all work. After dinner, during the hottest hours, Mr. Barnard rested and Niki went to Indian Pond. Usually he had it all to himself

for an hour or so. While he waited for his dinner to
digest, he liked to lie on the hot sand, looking into
the branches of a pine tree, discovering clusters of
fat cones, intricate patterns made by the needles, and
blobs of pitch that oozed from the rough bark. Small
brown birds flew in and out of the branches. Niki
wondered idly what they were. Above all was the sky
with a depth of blueness that was amazing as he lay
looking straight up into it. Fragrance of fern and pine
needles under the hot sun filled the air.

Oh boy, this was the life!

When he thought an hour had passed, he would
step into the warm shallows near the shore. It was a
beautiful place! Except for the cove where he stood,
the trees came close to the water's edge, every shade
of green, every shade of blue, in woods and water and
sky. And it was all his! So different from the crowded
tank at the Y. As he plunged into the deeper, colder
water, circling farther and farther beyond the raft, he
felt a tingling sense of freedom and exhilaration.

By two o'clock other boys and girls would arrive
for their afternoon fun. They were friendly. By the
end of the week Niki knew most of their names, and
a few began to stand out as individuals.

One boy, slim, red-headed, the fastest swimmer
on the pond, told Niki about his family's summer
camp where he had a fourteen-foot catboat. He prom-

ised to take Niki sailing. Another fellow, who came occasionally, had his own car and was apparently older than the others. He was quite a boy, a big talker. He spent most of his time chasing a girl who wore a yellow bathing suit, snatching her cap, or tipping her from the raft. All three were excellent swimmers. Niki finished a poor fourth when he joined their games and races. Joe, Toby, and June. Three names he was never to forget.

By mid-afternoon he was back at his hoeing. After supper he walked down the lane between fields of tall grass sweet with clover, bordered with delicate wild roses, enjoying the beauty of it, whistling in answer to the bob-white's call. As soon as he got the cows and milked them, his day's work was done.

One trip to the movies was enough. The theater was hot and stuffy, the walk to town and back was long after he had worked all day. Sometimes he got a ride down, and hung around the stores a while with other boys, treating them to ice cream and sodas, or playing the pinball machines. Occasionally, when it was very hot, he went for another swim after supper, but because half a dozen muscles ached whichever way he moved, it was good to sit quietly on the grass with Herky for company, and do nothing. It was so different from his life in the city, and yet he loved it.

Niki did a lot of thinking on those quiet evenings.

He thought back to Dziadziu, his Polish grandfather, who had come to America when he was no older than Niki, and who had overcome poverty, sickness, and loneliness, had learned the new language, married his pretty Irish sweetheart, and somehow or other earned enough money to buy a little piece of land. He had built his house himself, and planted his little garden, and all those years he had continued to work in the mill, riding ten miles a day on his bicycle, or walking when he couldn't ride.

Grandmother and Grandfather Louganis had had their hard times, too. His father was their only son, a brilliant student, intent upon becoming a doctor. They must have been awfully proud of him as he worked, studying nights, finishing school, and trying to get a college education. After he married Niki's mother, she worked so that he could spend all his time on his studies. Then came the war. He signed up for the Navy, was assigned to radar work on a destroyer. On its first trip out it was sunk by a Japanese submarine. Why? Why did there always have to be wars? Would he have to go, he wondered, and be killed like his father and Lewis?

As his thoughts swung back to himself, he felt only shame. He hadn't been very smart, falling for Deego and his gang. His father had been a serious student and a worker at his age. Dziadziu had been a man at fifteen. And Niki, what had he been doing? Dropping lighted matches in mailboxes, erasing the marks policemen put on tires and curbs to mark parking time, blocking the meters and vending machines with slugs. They weren't smart tricks. He knew it now.

That part of his life seemed a hundred years ago, and yet the horrible sound of screaming tires was with him still, and Deego's face, and Pete lying there on the grass . . .

Niki closed his eyes to shut out the memories, and turned his thoughts to the future, a future where he would have a farm and a chinchilla ranch. He could start as Mr. Barnard had, with three pairs, and have a herd worth more than twenty thousand dollars in four years. That was making money! And when he was rich, he would have a place exactly like this one, near a pond. He would have cows, too, and hens and a big garden. And a hired man to do the hoeing!

That was the end of his day. His eyes would not stay open. Bed and sleep were all that mattered, sleep in his own bed, in his own room.

But one evening an old truck with a mowing machine in tow rumbled into the yard. Niki was on his feet in a minute. It must be Sam Bumpus, the man they had been looking for to do the haying. Niki ran down to the barn to meet him. He found a tall, bony man who had more hair in his ears and on his shaggy, overhanging eyebrows than he had on the top of his head. Niki tagged along as the men walked towards the meadow.

"It don't pay to use a tractor on these small fields. Hoss and mowing machine's better," Sam explained.

"You'll surely come Monday?" Mr. Barnard asked.

"Eeyup. I can mow it all in one day. With a spell of good weather, you'll have it in the barn by the middle of the week."

"Can I help?" asked Niki.

"Sam will do the mowing, but you can help on the raking and loading."

Niki was pleased. It would be a lot better than hoeing. Anything was better than hoeing.

When they returned to the house, it was after nine. Mr. Barnard remembered that he had not fed the chinchillas and, seeing Niki's eager face, asked him to go along.

"Why do you feed them at night?" he asked.

"They can be fed any time, day or night. I used to feed them in the morning, but there were so many interruptions to that schedule that I changed to the evening feeding. I've got used to doing it this way. That's the only reason."

Preparations began in the kitchen. Mr. Barnard

took a pile of small plates and on each placed a leaf of kale, a bit of apple, and a few thin slices of carrot.

"Do they have salad every night?"

"No, not every night. There are many theories about the best diet for chinchillas, almost as many as there are breeders. I give mine a tablespoon of pellets, and alfalfa or clover hay, or timothy. I keep those things in the chinchilla house. But I think a bit of fresh vegetable is good for them once in a while."

Mr. Barnard gave some of the plates to Niki and took the rest himself. As they walked down the path together, Niki felt prickles of excitement. If he was really going to have a chinchilla ranch of his own some day, this was important, for it was preparing him for his life work. He watched carefully as Mr. Barnard opened a tin box that stood near the wall and measured a tablespoonful of small brownish pellets for each plate.

"What are they made of?"

"Choice grains, rice, corn, wheat, alfalfa, things like that, enriched with vitamins and minute quantities of trace minerals. Several commercial food companies make them. In fact the Kellogg Company that makes the cornflakes for your breakfast also makes pellets for chinchillas." While he was talking, Mr. Barnard opened a second box and put a handful of timothy hay beside the pellets on the plates.

He set the food inside the first cage. Niki watched every motion as the chinchillas picked up pieces of apple in their tiny forepaws and nibbled, watching him with their shiny black eyes, but continuing to nibble, undisturbed. First the salad disappeared. Then they began on the pellets.

"They certainly chew their food." Niki remained where he was, intent on seeing the whole dining process of that pair while Mr. Barnard placed the food in the other cages.

"They have sharp teeth," Mr. Barnard told him. "They are rodents, of course, and as you perhaps know, all rodents' teeth continue to grow. The log tunnels in their cages are for them to gnaw on, as well as for hiding places. And that round spool is salt."

"You certainly have everything for their comfort!"

"No, I haven't everything. There are much better cages than these on the market. I made my own. I read about what other breeders have, and then make the things I can't afford to buy."

Niki was ready with another question.

"What's the pop bottle with the glass tube for? Do they drink out of that thing?"

Apparently the boy's questions were endless, but Mr. Barnard found he didn't mind answering them.

"Yes," he said, "there's always a drop ready for them at the end of the tube."

"I wonder who thought up that invention."

"That I don't know, but it works all right. I wash and fill the bottles every day, and that's all there is to it. Of course the water has to be pure, not chlorinated, and ours is pure, because we have our own springs and pumping system."

"Look at this fellow nibble hay. He eats it like corn on the cob."

Man and boy watched together. At last, Mr. Barnard said, "Come on. It's getting late. They'll be eating for an hour yet, for they are nocturnal animals, but it's time for us farmers to go to bed."

"Which one is going to win the prize?"

Mr. Barnard laughed. "I didn't say just that, but it's this one. He the finest I've raised so far. His fur is unusual in quality and color. We breed for blue tones, blue-gray of course, but the bluer the better." They stopped at the center row of cages. "Come here, Hooper," Mr. Barnard called. "Come here and let the boy see you."

"Hello, Hooper. Sure and you're beautiful," Niki crooned, kneeling so that his face was on a level with the chinchilla's bright eyes. "Have they all got names?"

"Yes, names and pedigrees. I'll tell you about that sometime."

Niki laughed softly as he watched Hooper clean his whiskers with his tiny forepaws. Their paws looked so useless and under-developed, yet they were strong enough to help chinchillas cling to the side of the cage as they jumped around.

At last he stood up, brushing bits of hay from his knees. "He's pretty, all right," he said, "but they all look alike to me."

"They won't when you get to know them. See his mate over there? She's going to have her first baby in about a week."

"Boy, I'd love to see a baby. How big are they?"

"About two inches long. They're mostly head, but they're fully furred and have their eyes open. They can hop around almost as soon as they're born."

"How do you know the date?"

"Very often chinchillas breed again as soon as a baby is born. Then it's 111 days to the date of birth. Of course it can vary a few days either way, sooner or later. But this is Happy's first baby and she bred before I expected her to, so I can't be exactly sure in her case."

"Sometimes they have twins, don't they?"

"Occasionally three or four, or even five. Multiple births mean hand-feeding every two hours around the clock."

"I hope Happy will have three or four. Can I help feed them if she does?" The eagerness in Niki's voice touched a sore spot in Charles Barnard's heart.

"I think one will be enough for her this time. She's a temperamental female," he answered, collecting the things that were to go back to the house.

As they walked up the path Niki said, "I'm going to leave school as soon as I'm sixteen and get a job. How long do you suppose it will take to earn fifteen hundred dollars for my first pair?"

"You'll earn it faster if you finish high school first. By the way, did Mr. Morgan say anything about what I am to pay you?"

"No. He said it was this or reform school — and that I needn't expect to get paid for it."

Mr. Barnard snapped on the kitchen light. "I'll pay you what you're worth. It's up to you. I'll give you two dollars a week for spending money, and at the end of the summer I'll give you your pay in Savings Bonds. Considering everything, I think that's fair enough."

Niki watched as Mr. Barnard hung the key on a small hook beside the kitchen window. "I'll put it all towards the first pair. My spending money and everything. You're awfully good to me, and I'll prove that I deserve it."

When Niki had gone to his room, Mr. Barnard said to Martha, "You know, I think the boy is going to turn out all right. He certainly is interested in the chinchillas."

Martha looked up from her knitting.

"Oh, Charles, I'm so glad!" she said.

Chapter 5 SOMETHING TO WRITE HOME ABOUT

It was Sunday. The week's work was over. Except for the necessary chores of feeding the animals and milking, Sunday at the Barnards' was a day of rest.

In the city Niki had never known what to do with himself on Sundays. Deego usually had to work, and Jokey visited a married sister every Sunday. It had often seemed an endless day to Niki.

In the country, it was different. Breakfast was at eight. There was no need to hurry over the bacon with crisp French toast swimming in maple syrup, and as many of Mrs. Barnard's doughnuts as a boy could eat. Then, Niki attended church with the Barnards and, to please him, they drove around the long way home, over high hills and through neighboring villages. Dinner was at one. They were still sitting around the table discussing everything from politics to potato crops, when the clock struck two.

"This is nice, but it's not the way to get the dishes done," Mrs. Barnard said, beginning to stack the cups and saucers.

"That's just what my mother used to say," said Niki.

"Have you written to her?"

"I wrote the night I got here, and I'm going to write again today. The time goes so fast . . ."

"Tell us about your mother. What is she like?"

"Well," Niki hesitated. How could he describe her so that they would understand? It would have been easy to talk about his grandmother and make them laugh and enjoy the stories he could tell. But his mother was different. She worried over him. She irritated him. Yet he knew that with all her heart she loved him . . . but those weren't things he could say to the Barnards.

"Well," he began again, "there isn't anything to tell. She's thirty-eight. She's always saying she's too fat and that she's going to diet, but she doesn't do it. She likes to eat."

"Is she dark like you?"

"Her hair is brown but her eyes are blue, with flecks in them." (And tears in them, too, that morning when he had said goodbye.) Niki looked up to see the Barnards watching him, trying to read his thoughts. "She works in a real estate office," he went on quickly, "and ever since my father died, we've lived with my grandmother."

"Is the house in the city?"

"Yes." Niki sighed. "She sold the farm when my grandfather died. It's a small apartment, only four rooms. I sleep on a daybed in the living room."

"That's not so good," Mr. Barnard said. "Where do you do your homework?"

Niki grinned. "On the kitchen table, when I do any."

"Oh, I see." Mr. Barnard's voice showed disapproval.

"You sounded just like Mr. Morgan then," Niki said. He guessed all teachers were alike when it came to homework. His face grew serious as he continued, "But I've always worked in study periods. I really plug. I've always had good marks until this past term. Next year I'll get all A's and B's."

"You went to pieces in a big way last term?"

"Yes, I guess I did."

"Just what happened?"

Niki didn't want to talk about it. He traced a pattern on the tablecloth with his finger before answering, "I don't know."

Mr. Barnard studied the boy's face. "It takes a strong character to go with bad company and come through unscathed. That was how the trouble started, wasn't it, bad company? Mr. Morgan told me something about it, but I'd like to hear your story."

There was a long silence. Niki thought of Jokey . . . he was a good pal, not bad company. Suddenly he seemed to see his face as they had stood with the group in the police station, frightened, their nerve gone, caught in a snarl of lies. And he himself had lied, too, just as fast as any of them. He had hated himself even while he was doing it, but still he had lied because the others did.

He wet his lips and faced Mr. Barnard. "We got into trouble all right, but I learned my lesson. I'm through with that kind of stuff. Next year I'm going to make good. I've got to so Mr. Morgan won't be sorry he gave me the chance to come here."

"That's a noble resolution," Mr. Barnard said as he pushed back his chair. He put a friendly arm across Niki's shoulders. "Stick to it, boy."

Niki was so pleased with himself that he stopped in the kitchen and offered to help Mrs. Barnard with the dishes.

"Bless you, no," she said. "Go down to the pond and have a nice swim with your friends."

Niki needed no urging. When he reached the pond he looked in vain for Joe or June, but Toby was there. Niki was pleased when the older boy called to him, "Hi, Niki, race you to Table Rock."

"Where's that?"

"Across the pond."

"Okay. Let's go." Niki had never tried the long swim before, but he took the challenge willingly. Before he was halfway across he was sorry, for Toby outdistanced him easily, without a backward look.

Niki's arms and legs ached, and it seemed as though his heart and lungs would burst with the effort to keep going. He remembered the big chicken dinner he had just eaten. If he had cramps or became exhausted, he could drown before anybody could help. He lifted his head and saw Toby walking ashore. He had never disliked anybody as much as he did Toby at that moment.

Niki floated and managed to tread water a few minutes until his heart stopped pounding so hard, then finished the distance and climbed onto the large rock where Toby was lying face down, sunning himself.

"I wondered where you'd been all afternoon,"

Toby said with a sneering laugh. He moved over to make room for Niki. "What's the matter? You look all in."

"I'm all right."

"That's good, because I've got to go. I'm going to help a friend of mine fix up his jalopy for a hot rod race. Ever been to one?"

"Sure."

"Last week I made eighty-five dollars."

"You mean you raced?" Niki looked up with sudden admiration in his eyes. It took nerve to race those wrecks around a track.

"No. I placed bets on a sure thing. If you've got a couple of bucks, I can cut you in on something."

Niki hesitated. Toby's remarks had a familiar ring. Pete and Deego used to get the dope on "sure things." Sometimes they made money; oftener, they lost. If he was going to save for a chinchilla ranch, he'd better hang on to his two dollars.

"No, thanks," he said.

"Okay, kid, it's up to you," Toby said as he plunged into the water.

Niki was glad to have him go. Knowing there was no one to taunt him, he took his time swimming back to the cove. He made it easily, and felt pleased with himself as he rubbed down and put on his slacks and shirt. He determined to swim across every day and strengthen his muscles as he worked for speed.

On the way home, he kept thinking about Toby. Perhaps he had misjudged him. After all, he had no way of knowing that all Niki's swimming had been done in an indoor pool. He probably meant all right. Still, the feeling of dislike persisted.

He found Mr. Barnard on the porch, reading the Sunday paper.

"Have a good swim?" he asked.

"Yes. Across the pond and back. I'm improving." Then, as Mr. Barnard laid aside the paper, Niki asked, "If you're not too busy, will you answer a few questions about the chinchillas? I'm going to write to my mother and Mr. Morgan, and there are some things I need to know."

"Such as what?"

"What's in those nesting boxes? I mean do they build a nest like rabbits do, or like squirrels?"

"No, no nests. The boxes are empty."

"Do you suppose Happy has had her baby yet?"

"No, not yet."

Niki balanced his long body on the porch rail, and viewed his sunburned arms with admiration.

"Did you name them, and if you sold them to somebody else would he keep the names they have

now, or call them something different? And all those
letters and numbers on the cards on the cages, what
do they mean?"

Mr. Barnard laughed as he laid down the paper
and rose to his feet. "Come on, Niki. Such a marvelous
thirst for information must be satisfied. I'll get the
key."

"These are the cards I meant," Niki exclaimed as
soon as they were inside the chinchilla house. "Dolly,
Dinky, Chica, Ande, Smoky, Susy, Happy, Hooper.
Then the letters CLB. Those are your initials, aren't
they?"

"It's called a ranch number, but it really is a
brand. Each chinchilla has the ranch number tattooed
on his left ear. Every new rancher must choose a
combination of letters not already registered for anybody else."

"Tattooed? You mean they prick it through his
skin? I should think it would hurt," Niki interrupted,
looking carefully at Smoky. "This one's tattooed on
both ears."

"They all are. The letter on the right ear tells the
year the animal was born, and the number is his own
individual number."

"There's a lot to it, isn't there?"

"There is to anything worth while."

Niki returned to the card and read it aloud.

```
CLB, Smoky  M Z4
dam CLB X  litter 1M
sire CLB V          1F
    5/21/53
```

"What does it mean?"

"We use letters instead of numbers to save space. Chinchillas' ears are pretty small, you know. The year 1955 is B; 1954 was A; 1953 was Z; 1952, X; 1951, V; 1950, T; and so on. The card means that Smoky's dam was born on my ranch in 1952; his sire was born here in 1951. The date May 21, 1953, is the date when Smoky was born."

"You say there's a B and an A, but at the end of the alphabet you skipped some letters. Why was that?"

"W takes up a lot of room, and U and Y might easily be confused with V."

"Oh. It says Z4. What's the 4 for?" Niki asked, intent on knowing all the answers.

"The 4 means that he was the fourth animal born on my ranch that year. In the house I have a card catalog with the history of all the breedings and off-spring. Every animal is graded, too, and then registered with the Chinchilla Association of America."

"What's grading?"

"It's an inspection done by a professional. They

are graded and rated on size and shape of head, neck,
body; on the color and quality of fur, and the shading
or veiling pattern. We're breeding for bluish tints,
and uniformity of size and quality."

"How long before you can sell the pelts?"

"In a year or two, maybe longer. The market is
constantly changing. Today, quality is the only thing
that counts. There is almost no sale for inferior
animals, either for breeding or pelts. A prize pair
can still bring fifteen hundred dollars or more, but a
pair can be bought for as little as fifty dollars. Anybody can raise chinchillas today, but a man's got to
be a specialist to make any money in the business."

"It must take a lot of pelts to make a coat."

"It does — two hundred fifty or more — and
they must match perfectly before they can be used by
a furrier."

"I bet those coats cost something!"

"Twenty to thirty thousand dollars. At present
the skins that are sold are usually made into capes or
shoulder wraps, mostly for advertising. I've read
somewhere that there are only forty full-length coats
in the world. Most of them belong to Hollywood
stars and other rich and glamorous ladies."

"Where did they get theirs?"

"They were made before the current ban on selling pelts went into effect. So many animals were

killed that they were practically extinct when Chapman went to South America."

"I read about him." As Niki walked from cage to cage, he thought about Matthias Chapman, the mining engineer from Oregon, who brought the first chinchillas to this country.

Early in 1918, when Chapman was working at an isolated camp high in the Andes Mountains, he heard Indian trappers talk about chinchillas and their soft, thick fur. He asked to see one, but the trappers said so many had been killed for their pelts that they were very hard to find.

At last a trapper did find one. For two weeks he carried it around in a five-gallon can, feeding it fresh grass every day, and then, upon returning to Mr. Chapman's camp, made him a present of it. It was a poor, half-starved little creature, but Matthias Chapman was impressed with the fact that it had managed to live that long with so little care. He began to wonder if the pretty animals could be raised in captivity.

By that time, the South American countries had passed laws forbidding the trapping of chinchillas, but Chapman, by special permission, sent out twenty trappers. It took them three years, but at the end of that time there were a dozen healthy chinchillas in the cages he had built for them.

His troubles weren't over, however, for South America had passed more laws, forbidding the export of animals or pelts. Again, Chapman worked to get permission to transport his to the United States. All this time he had to watch patiently over the animals because the change from the cool, dry climate of the Andes Mountains to the hot climate of the lowlands was hard on them. At last the necessary permission was granted. On the long trip up the coast of South America, the cages were cooled with cakes of ice. On the steamship that took them to Los Angeles, he kept them in his own stateroom so he could watch over them constantly. All that work for a dozen chinchillas, Niki thought, and it took 250 of them to make a coat!

"Does it ever get too hot for them here?" he asked. While he was talking he watched Chica sit up like a miniature kangaroo, while Ande jumped around the wire sides of the cage like a little monkey.

"Yes. They can stand the cold all right, but they faint — really pass out — if it gets too hot. I wet down the roof with the hose in very hot weather, and if the water supply gets low, and it does all too often when we go for weeks without rain, I use electric fans blowing over cakes of ice. Any temperature above ninety is bad in a chinchilla house."

Mr. Barnard opened the door of Dinky's cage

and picked him up by his stiff little tail, holding him in one hand while he stroked him with the other.

"Feel that fur," he told Niki. "Chinchillas sometimes have as many as eighty hairs in each follicle where a rabbit has only one. These little fellows never have fleas or lice. Their fur is so thick that insect pests would smother."

"Sure and you're the softest thing in the world," Niki whispered. "It's as though I was touching nothing but air. Well, I suppose there wouldn't be any any reason for raising them if you couldn't sell the fur, but it doesn't seem right to me to put 250 of them into a coat for a dame."

Mr. Barnard blew on the deep fur so that it parted in a perfect circle. "No other fur will do that," he said.

"It's pretty the way every hair is shaded to make the little dark circle and the white circle, and yet they look all gray."

"That's what counts in grading, the way the hair shades from the dark tip through the white band to the bluish tones underneath."

Mr. Barnard held Dinky on his hand a minute longer before opening the door of the cage and replacing him gently on the sugar cane litter that covered the floor.

"You picked him up by the tail when you took

him out," Niki said. "I should think that might hurt him."

"His bones are so tiny you could crush them if he struggled to get away, or if you dropped him. I think the tail lift is the best method when you are catching hold of one. Well," he smiled at Niki, "is that enough for one day?"

"It sure is. Thanks. I've got enough in my head to fill a dozen letters. Mr. Morgan and my mother will know something about chinchillas before I get through!"

Niki felt an exultation that nearly swept him off his feet as he dashed up the stairs to his room. Not only would he have the chinchillas to write about, but he could also tell his mother and Mr. Morgan that he had made the grade. Mr. Barnard liked him!

Chapter 6 **STUPID THING TO DO**

Clackety clackety clack, clackety clackety clack; gee, whoa; clackety clackety clack, the rhythm of the old mowing machine sounded in Niki's ears. He stopped hoeing and leaned on the fence to watch the long blade cut an even swath around the field. With each turn the square of standing grass diminished, until all was mown. Throughout the day and far into the evening, the clackety clack continued. When Sam Bumpus finally called it a day, every field was mown.

The next morning he returned with another machine. Niki jumped the fence the first time Sam stopped to rest his horse.

"What do you call that thing?" he asked eagerly.

"Tedder."

"It kicks the hay so it will dry faster?"

"EEyup."

Niki looked up at the great head and shoulders of the shaggy brown horse. "What's his name?" he asked.

"Daisy."

"Will she bite?"

"Nope."

"Hello, Daisy, you're a good old horse," said Niki, patting her long neck.

Daisy swung her head around and nudged him between the shoulders. Niki jumped a mile.

"Ain't used to hosses?"

Niki grinned. "No, I've never had a chance to drive one, but I'd like to. I bet I could drive the tedder. Mr. Barnard said I could help with the haying."

"Get aboard. Nothin' could happen to you drivin' Daisy. She wouldn't run if she was struck by lightnin'."

Mr. Bumpus stood by silently as Niki climbed into the small iron seat and experimented with the hand lever. Then, picking up the reins, he persuaded Daisy to move. Happiness glowed through him. He was a man, a farmer! He felt on that morning that all the world belonged to him.

The hot summer sun beat on his bare back; the hot, sweet smell of drying clover filled the air. Insects buzzed loudly and birds hopped about the field. Niki loved it. He and his horse Daisy ran the tedder all that day until the red sun sank in the west.

Even with gunny sacks for padding, the small seat had grown harder and smaller as the hours passed. Niki was so lame he could hardly move, but the good feeling of elation lasted. As soon as he had cleaned up and changed his clothes, he announced that he was going to the drug store to buy some film.

"Wait until tomorrow. I'll be going down and I'll get them for you," said Mr. Barnard. "You've done enough for one day."

"I wish you would take my picture driving Daisy. I've been meaning to get film for a long time. I want your picture, too, and Mrs. Barnard, and Herky, and the chinchillas. I want to send some to my mother and Mr. Morgan."

"That reminds me. You had a card in the evening mail."

Niki's mother wrote to him often, but this card was a surprise, for it was from Jokey. He was doing all right in the garage, and getting fifteen dollars a week besides his board and room.

"Good for Jokey," Niki said, as he read it aloud. "I'll send him a set of pictures, too. He can have his city job. I'm glad I got the country."

"If you're determined to get those films tonight, I'll drive you down in the car. I'll be glad to take your picture with Daisy, but tomorrow I want you to help Mrs. Barnard with some canning. Those peas and strawberries are going to waste. She can't do it alone, but she can tell you what to do."

A slow flush colored Niki's face. His eyes narrowed; he bit his lips. He — who could drive a horse, and ted, and rake, and even load hay with a little help from Sam Bumpus — he wasn't going to stay in the kitchen and can strawberries. What did they expect?

"Why tomorrow? Why can't it wait until the haying is done?" He tried to keep his voice patient and reasonable.

"With this hot weather they'll be gone, Niki. You can help me in the morning and drive the horse in the afternoon," Mrs. Barnard answered gently.

Niki was tired, dog tired. His dreams tumbled and shattered completely. A red surge of anger rose to his face.

"Okay," he shouted. "I work from morning to

night, and you load on more work and more work.
You needn't get any car. I'll walk." And slamming
the door as hard as he could, he started for the drug-
store.

All the way to town and back, Niki thought about
the canning. He might as well be a slave, working all
day long, and no pay unless he did exactly what Mr.
Barnard asked. He wished he had a job like Jokey's,
getting fifteen bucks a week. Here he had no friends,
no fun, no nothing. It was absolutely the deadest
town in the state. Gosh, but he wished he were back
in the city.

His feet dragged as he climbed the hill. He
walked slowly and more slowly as he approached the
house. "Down, Hercules, get down," he snarled as
the boxer came to meet him. When the dog obeyed
his command, Niki felt lonelier still.

The black mood was still with him as he entered
the kitchen. He found Mr. Barnard there, seated at
the table with a bedtime snack of milk and cookies.

"Join me, Niki?" he asked pleasantly. "Did you
get your film?"

"I got it. Anything more you want to know?"
Niki's sullen eyes met Mr. Barnard's in a vain attempt to stare him down.

"No," he replied, very quietly. "But there is
something you must remember, Nikolas. Unless you

are courteous and willing to do what we ask you to do, you will go back to Mr. Morgan on the next train. That's all. Good night."

Niki's face flushed with anger as he turned and left the room.

The following morning he picked peas, and helped Mrs. Barnard shell and can them. He worked silently and unsmilingly. Although he enjoyed his first experience with a pressure cooker, he was determined not to show it. By ten o'clock a dozen pint jars stood on the shelf, filled to the top with bright green peas.

Mrs. Barnard's face was pinker than usual as she asked, "Will you pick the strawberries now, Niki? Charles is going to take me down to get some more wax for the glasses. It won't take long to make jam, and think how good it will taste on hot biscuits."

Niki did not answer. A hot wave of resentment swept over him. They had planned it this way, on purpose to show him he must obey. For a while he worked at the slow business of filling boxes with small, late berries, his mind full of bitter thoughts. The day was hot and muggy, and he was tired and sore from yesterday's long hours on the tedder. Over in the meadow Sam Bumpus was raking hay, a job he had promised Niki could do. Niki had no desire to talk to him or anybody.

He went to the kitchen for another drink of water. As he washed his sticky hands, he looked at the small key hanging beside the window. Why not take a look at the chinchillas? Nobody would ever know. He was entitled to something to make up for being kitchen police all day. Maybe Happy had her baby by now. There was only one way to find out!

He spoke quietly to Hercules, unlocked the door of the chinchilla house, and went in. He fed Hooper a piece of clover, but no amount of coaxing would persuade Happy to leave her nesting box.

"I'll be back, Happy," he said. "I'll be keeping an eye on you." Sure, he had done it once, easy, and he would do it again every chance he got. Why not? There was no reason why he shouldn't. It was just Mr. Barnard's old school-teacher bossiness thinking nobody could take care of chinchillas except himself. Anyway, what he didn't know wouldn't bother him.

When the Barnards returned, they helped Niki pick more berries and hull them, but it was late afternoon before the last kettle of seething hot fruit was ladled into sterilized glasses. Niki still had a sink full of dirty dishes to do. No time to swim, no chance to drive Daisy and ride the hayrake. Just work, work, work. Woman's work! How he hated it!

After the cows were milked, he ran them to the

pasture and, dressed in bathing trunks, jeans and a shirt, hurried to the pond. After a swim he would go somewhere. He deserved some fun, he thought, looking resentfully at the strawberry stains on his hands.

It was good to swim across the pond and back. When he climbed onto the raft to rest, he found Joe there. Niki liked Joe, but found it hard to understand him. He wasn't like Toby, that was sure, and yet he seemed always to be with him and June. If it was June he liked, he seemed to be a very patient tagger-on, not half trying to win. Joe was a lot smaller than Toby, and younger, but June didn't have much sense, Niki concluded, if she couldn't appreciate his superior qualities. It was no compliment to call a boy a gentleman, according to Niki's standards, but somehow Joe was a gentleman without there being one sissy thing about him.

Having thought all those thoughts, and having caught his breath after his long swim, Niki rolled over.

"I'll be glad if I can ever swim as easy as you do, Joe," he said.

"I've been doing it since I was three years old. We've always had a camp on the woods side of Robbins' Pond, and I guess I could swim almost as soon as I could walk. I'd like to take you over to our place. It's three miles in through the woods, just a little place. I sleep outdoors unless it rains. Did you ever do that?"

Niki hadn't, and Joe went on, "We're going over tonight to take an extra tent and supplies for Fourth of July weekend. Want to ride over? We're coming right back."

"Yes, I'd like to."

"Do you have to let the Barnards know?" Joe asked, and again Niki recognized the quality of thoughtfulness or whatever it was that made Joe different.

"No," Niki replied and he thought, let them worry a little. Maybe they would appreciate him more when he came back.

"Okay. Stay near the raft so I can find you." With strong, effortless strokes Joe cut across the pond.

Niki stayed on the raft because he saw June's yellow cap heading his way. Behind her, as usual, was Toby. As she pulled herself up onto the raft, she called back to him, "Toby, I'll go if Niki does."

"Go where?" Niki asked, wondering what she was talking about.

"To the movies with Toby," she said, running her fingers through her dripping hair.

"Not me," Niki said emphatically. "It's too hot
for movies."

Toby spoke, hanging onto the raft by his fingers.
"Not to that sweat-box in town. We're going to the
Drive-In. It's about twelve miles out on the State Road.
Want to go?" It was a grudging invitation. Niki won-
dered why he made it.

"Answer's still no," he said. "I'm going to Joe's
camp in a few minutes."

"Oh, you can go there any time," said June,
smiling at him. He noticed with surprise her big,
brown eyes and long, dark lashes. He wasn't quite so
sure after that what he wanted to do.

"Joe," June called as he circled towards them,
"we're going to the movies in Toby's car."

"You are not," said Joe.

"We are too. Niki's going with us because I
asked him."

Joe looked at Niki and shrugged. "Okay, if that's
the way you want it." He turned to Toby. "Get her
home by eleven, if you know what's good for you,
and good for her, too. Stupid!" He addressed the last
word to June, and swam away.

Niki couldn't understand it, but before the evening was over he knew Joe's parting word applied to
him. Everything he did was stupid — insisting on

paying their way in, and treating to ice cream cones, cokes, and popcorn. June sat between him and Toby, and every time Niki felt her arm press against his, and every time he saw those long, dark lashes and her amazing eyes, he did another stupid thing. When Toby boasted that he was paid forty dollars a week for working on the greens at the golf course, Niki told them that including his board, he was doing better than that at the Barnards'. Not for worlds would he have June or Toby suspect that this one evening had cost him every cent he had or would have for a week.

Apparently the time meant nothing to June, and they saw the picture through. When Toby left Niki at the Barnards' drive, Niki told him to remember what June's red-headed boy friend had said, and to take her straight home.

Toby scowled at him, but June laughed as she reached out and caught Niki's hand.

"Didn't you know?" she asked. "Joe isn't my boy friend. He's my twin brother."

The dark shadow of Toby's arm lay across her shoulders as they drove away. Niki wasn't exactly sure why it mattered, but he kept thinking about it, and he didn't like it.

He let himself in quietly and set the night latch. There was a light in the Barnards' room, but he passed without speaking. His anger towards them had burned itself out, replaced now with anger and disgust towards himself. Of all the dumb things a fellow could do, he hadn't missed one. He'd spent every cent he had. Mournfully he searched the empty pockets of his jeans. He had lost the friendship of the boy he wanted most to know, the boy who was June's brother.

"Crazy nut," he mumbled as he kicked off his shoes.

All night long his thoughts whirled round and round, changing to fitful dreams where Joe, Toby, and brown-eyed June stood looking at him and saying, "Stupid."

Chapter 7 HOOPER

In the morning Niki did what had to be done quickly. He went directly to Mr. Barnard.

"I'm sorry about getting in late last night. I went to the Drive-In theater, but I thought we'd be back by eleven. Next time I will tell you before I go."

Mr. Barnard said briefly, "Please do, or there will never be another next time."

Niki smiled his old ingratiating smile. "Okay, boss," he said.

It was a good day! He got his chance to help with the haying, and Sam Bumpus took his picture raking, loading, and leading Daisy by her halter. Not until after supper was there time for a swim. He felt unusual excitement as he ran down to the pond.

There was no sign of Toby and June. Joe gave him a short hello. He started to swim across the pond, and turned to find June following him.

"Did you get home all right last night?" he asked.

"Of course. Followed by the usual furor, only worse. I had no idea it was getting late. My father says I can't go out with Toby any more. But I don't care."

"He should have seen that you got home at eleven the way Joe said."

They climbed onto Table Rock. June took off her cap and shook her pretty yellow hair over her shoulders. It was dry tonight, and fluffy as spun gold. Niki couldn't stop looking at it, and her.

"How did you happen to go to the Barnards' to work?" she asked.

"Well, you see it was like this," Niki began slowly, intensely aware that only three inches separated him from a beautiful, brown-eyed doll, and that she liked him. "Mr. Barnard wanted somebody to help him with his chinchillas. The principal of my school is a friend of Charlie Barnard's. He's a good friend of mine, too." He paused, enjoying the knowl-

edge that that much, at least, was true. "Mr.
Morgan knew I was interested in breeding chinchillas,
so he wrote to Charlie and recommended me."

He smiled at June, and she smiled back. He wig-
gled his toes with happiness and ruffled her hair so
that the setting sun shone through the gold.

"Do you know a lot about them?" she asked,
pushing her hair into place primly, and moving one-
and-a-half inches farther away.

"I ought to. I take care of them all the time,"
Niki boasted.

"I'd love to see them. What do they look like?"

"Something like squirrels. They sit up like kan-
garoos."

"Really?" June's attention was flattering, stimu-
lating Niki to new efforts.

"They are rodents, you know, herbivorous animals, nocturnal in their habits," he said impressively.
Not for nothing had he spent his time reading the
magazines!

Her eyes opened wider.

"High altitudes in the Andes are their natural
habitat. The only place in the world where they've
been found is in that region of South America, Chile,
Peru, Bolivia, Argentina, where there are warm days
and cold nights, and a cold, dry climate." He hoped
it sounded sensible, and that he'd hit the right coun-

tries, but probably she would never know the difference anyway.

"No kidding!" June opened her big, beautiful eyes until they were bigger, browner, and more beautiful than ever, and fluttered her long lashes until Niki felt a responding flutter in the region where his heart was supposed to be, but even that did not interrupt his discourse.

"I've made quite a study of chinchillas and their habits. Some day I'll tell you about the man who first brought them to this country. Did you know they cost as much as fifteen hundred dollars a pair?"

"Oh, Niki, no! You're wonderful. You know so much!"

"No, there's nothing wonderful about it," he said, with a patronizing smile.

"Are they in cages?"

"Naturally. A pair to a cage. Each cage is about thirty-six inches long, twenty-four high, by twenty deep." He measured off the distances with his hands. "They are made of wire, with two inches of sugar cane litter on the floor, like chips, and there is a nesting box on each cage, and a hollow log for them to gnaw on and play in."

There was awe in June's face as she said, "Wasn't Mr. Barnard lucky to get you because you know all about them!"

With such an appreciative audience, Niki could hardly stop to catch his breath. He wanted to tell her all he knew, to be wonderful, more wonderful, most wonderful.

"Each cage has a bottle of drinking water with a tube attached, and they sit up and drink from it."

She was speechless, so he continued, "We feed the mothers and babies Pablum."

"Niki, you're making it all up!"

"I am not. It's true, every word I've said. And their fur is so soft and fine you can't feel it."

"Oh, Niki, I want to see them. Will you show them to me? Now?"

"Sure. Do you suppose we can climb this bank? It's nearer."

She was away like a flash, and Niki after her, digging his bare toes into the slippery pine needles, grabbing at branches to pull himself up the steep places, and scrambling through underbrush that scratched at his feet and legs. He chased her across the road to the Barnards' driveway where she stopped, because Hercules came galloping down to see who was there.

"This is June, Hercules. She's a friend," Niki explained in introducton. "Hercules is a thorough-bred boxer, trained to attack strangers. We never worry about our animals when he is on guard. He would tear anybody to pieces, if they tried to steal our chinchillas."

June kept as far away from the dangerous animal as she could.

"Hello, anybody home?" Niki called.

There was no answer. The car was not in the garage. Probably the Barnards had gone for a short evening ride. The only question: When would they get back?

"Aren't you going to show them to me?" June asked.

"Just a minute." Why not? He could do it quickly. He knew where the key hung. The door was never locked. He was glad the Barnards were gone.

Proudly, he opened the door of the chinchilla house. "There they are. Fifty thousand dollars worth!"

"Aren't they cute! I want to touch one."

"No. I can't let you do that."

"Oh, Niki, please. I won't go one step until you let me hold one." She stuck her finger through the wire and Dinky nibbled at it.

Niki thought of all the reasons why he shouldn't open the cage door but, after all, they were only Mr. Barnard's reasons. Dinky and Dolly were all over their cage. One might escape while he was grabbing its mate. But he believed he could take Hooper out

safely, for Happy seldom ventured out of her nesting
box.

"This is Hooper, our most valuable animal," he
said, opening the cage door. After a few unsuccessful
grabs, he caught him by the tail. But instead of
nestling down in Niki's hands, the little fellow struggled desperately to get away. It seemed as though his
excitement spread to all the cages.

Niki talked softly to the frightened animal. "It's
all right, Hooper. Nobody's going to hurt you. Feel
how soft his fur is, June."

"Some day I'm going to have a coat like that."

"It will cost you twenty-five or thirty thousand
dollars."

"Let me take him," she coaxed, holding out her
hands.

"Be careful. Don't squeeze him," Niki cautioned
her.

Just what happened next, he never knew. Hooper
was on the floor. June was screaming, "He bit me!"
and running towards the door.

"Stand still. Don't you dare open that door," Niki
shouted.

June stood still. Around the room dashed Hooper.
Niki, his hands trembling, his heart pounding in his
chest, began to doubt whether he could ever catch the
little fugitive. All the other animals were dashing

around the sides of their cages. Even Happy came out to see what was going on.

At last Niki grabbed the terrified Hooper, not by the tail, but firmly around his body. On the tip of the tiny nose was one red drop of blood. Niki rubbed it away with his finger. As gently as possible he replaced him in his cage, fastened it, pushed June out the door, locked it, and returned the key to its hook beside the kitchen window.

He sat down on the steps because his knees were shaking so he had to. He mopped cold sweat from his face.

"Don't you ever tell anybody I let you in there. If Hooper is hurt it will cost me my job, and Mr. Barnard could sue your father for a thousand dollars, because you dropped him."

"I didn't mean to." June's eyes were wide with fright.

"Let's get out of here. I want my shoes and towel."

It seemed strange that everything at the pond was just as before. It seemed to Niki that it was hours ago they had left it. He picked up his things, and with one parting warning to June, returned home, his thoughts in a turmoil.

When the Barnards got back, Niki, saying he was tired, went to his room. He knew he ought to tell Mr.

Barnard, but he couldn't say the words. He sat listening, waiting, while Mr. Barnard made his nightly trip to feed the chinchillas; listening, waiting, until he returned to the house.

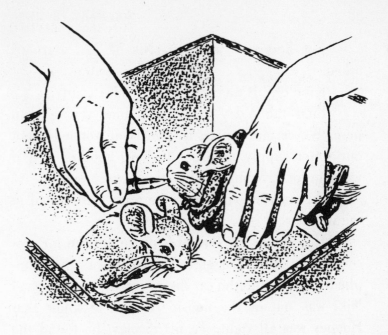

Chapter 8 **NIKI'S TWINS**

All night long Niki heard the grandfather clock boom out the hours. He heard the roosters crow and the early morning twittering of the birds. It was a sunless dawn in keeping with his thoughts. The wind rose and soon pelting rain beat against the east windows.

He tried to eat breakfast as usual. He tried to read Mr. Barnard's face when he returned from a trip to the chinchilla house. He tried to put his heart into cleaning the cellar, a job which had been planned for this rainy day. He felt light-headed and heavy-hearted as he went through the motions.

"Not homesick are you, Niki?" Mr. Barnard asked.

"Kind of." It was as good an excuse as any.

"First rainy day we've had since you've been here. We certainly need it. I've been worried about our water supply. I've got to have another well if we're in for dry summers like these every year."

Niki made no comment. He wasn't interested in the weather.

After dinner the Barnards drove to town for gro-ceries, and to take eggs to the customers they sup-plied. The minute the car disappeared down the road Niki was out of the house. He had to know that Hooper was all right. To his dismay, he found the little fellow in a separate cage, huddled in the corner. Niki knelt in front of it.

"Hooper, are you all right? Come over and see me."

Hooper did not budge. His ears looked droopy, his eyes, glassy. He looked as miserable as Niki felt. Could it be broken ribs or dislocated bones? Had he injured his sensitive mouth or nose? A sharp pain throbbed in Niki's head as he remembered . . . . He would have given a million dollars, if he'd had it, to have that chinchilla leap up on the wire just once.

Suddenly Niki's attention was diverted to the cage where Happy had been left alone. What in the

world was the matter with her? She was dashing
around, jumping against the wire, then rushing to the
farthest corner of the cage. Niki looked closer and
could hardly believe his eyes, for there, in the corner
was a tiny bit of fur that moved as Happy nipped it.

"Gosh, it's a baby! Stop it, Happy. Don't you
know it's your own baby? What do you think you're
doing?" He poked at her with his finger and she
leaped away. The poor little mite in the corner
seemed more dead than alive.

A second baby poked its head from the nesting
box. Happy paid no attention to it, but again tumbled
the first baby around in the sugar cane chips that
covered the floor.

Niki shivered. What should he do? He could open
the cage and rescue the babies, but his being in the
chinchilla house to do it would require a lot of explaining. And it would inevitably lead to the dis-
covery of his earlier visit, and Niki felt more sure
than ever that once Mr. Barnard found out about
June and Hooper, it would mean the end of everything as far as Niki was concerned. The best thing to
do, he decided, was to get out of there. Yes. It was
the only safe thing to do. Sit tight and say nothing.
He would be all right unless June squealed. As he
hung the key on its hook, he knew it was the most
cowardly decision he had ever made in his life.

Again he went to work in the cellar. It was no use. He put his finger against his throat where the pulse pounded so hard it hurt. He felt sick to his stomach and went upstairs to get a drink of water.

As soon as he entered the kitchen he knew why he had come. No matter what the consequences might be, he was going to save those babies. He gulped down the water, took the key from its hook, and hurried out into the yard.

His hands trembled as he unlocked the doors, stepped inside and closed them again. He put the small carrying cage on top of the feed boxes and opened its door. Then he walked to Happy's cage. She was in the nesting box, so he opened the door quickly, reached in and scooped up a handful of litter and the smaller baby with it. It was such a tiny furry body. He placed it in the carrying cage and went back for the other one.

Catching it was not so easy. For a long time it stayed in the nesting box, and Happy stayed out. Niki watched and coaxed and hoped with all his heart that the Barnards would not come back and find him in there. At last his patience was rewarded. The baby came out and as Niki reached for it, Happy ran into her nest again. He put the second baby with the other one.

He stopped long enough to look for Hooper, but although Niki tapped on the wires and called his name, Hooper stayed out of sight. Again Niki felt the cold fear, the tight twist in his stomach. Something was wrong. He ought to tell Mr. Barnard about the accident so the veterinarian could make an examination and find out where the little fellow was hurt. He must tell Mr. Barnard . . . tell him everything . . . as soon as he got home.

With a sigh from the depths of his troubled heart, Niki locked the doors and went to work again. He had to work now, the harder the better, to relieve the tension that was tying him in knots. He washed the windows. He swept and scrubbed the cement floor.

The minute he heard the Barnards' car he ran to meet it. He wet his lips and swallowed the lump in his throat.

"What's the matter, Niki? You look as though you'd seen a ghost," Mr. Barnard said, as he stopped the car.

Niki told his story, haltingly at first, but the words tumbled over one another as he described what he had seen.

"And then I put them in an empty cage," he concluded, "because I couldn't just stand there and see her hurting them. She would have killed that littlest one, Mr. Barnard, if I hadn't rescued it. I know I shouldn't have gone in without you, but no matter what you do to me, I'm glad I did it."

Niki felt it was a good climax. Would he get thanks for a good deed, or would he get his ticket home? He concentrated on Mrs. Barnard, realizing she would help him if she could.

She looked anxiously from the boy to her husband. Then she touched his sleeve. "Charles, Niki probably saved their lives."

"Perhaps. But I don't want a boy around whom I can't trust. How many times have you been in there before this?"

"Twice before."

"I'm glad you tell the truth."

The lump tightened in Niki's throat. This was the time to tell the whole truth and get it off his chest. But the words wouldn't come.

Niki unloaded groceries while Mr. Barnard went into the chinchilla house. He had the small carrying cage in his hand when he returned to the kitchen.

"Go down to Brock's farm and get a pint of goat's milk."

"Yes, sir." Niki flew as though he had wings on his heels.

Before Mrs. Barnard had the groceries put away,

he was back. He watched Mr. Barnard warm the milk, test it for temperature, and fill a tiny medicine dropper half full. He opened the cage and placed both babies in a deep carton. Then with a large, soft washcloth in his hand, he picked up the livelier baby and enclosed it in the cloth. As soon as he touched its mouth with the warm milk, it began to drink.

When it was the weaker baby's turn, the response was not so good.

"It's going to be all right, though, I think," Mr. Barnard said. "It took a few drops."

Niki watched in silence. What a wonderful thing he was seeing. The beginning of life, a life he had saved.

Looking up, Mr. Barnard caught the expression in the boy's eyes. He could appreciate the curiosity and burning interest that had made Niki go in to look for Happy's baby. He knew it had taken real courage to save the baby's life and own up to his wrongdoing.

"Well," he said, "they're your twins. What are you going to name them?"

Niki could hardly believe he had heard the words correctly.

"I don't know yet," he said.

"Be thinking about it. I want you to take care of

them. But you must promise me now, on your word of honor, that you will never go into the chinchilla house again without permission."

"I promise."

"A promise is to keep, Niki," Mr. Barnard said, looking at him steadily with kindly, searching eyes. He extended his hand and Niki took it. Then he hung the key in its old place beside the kitchen window.

Niki's heart swelled with gratitude. Words pounded in his head . . . Oh, Mr. Barnard, there's something I want to tell you . . . tell you . . . tell you . . .

"Good luck to you and your twins, my boy."

So the moment for telling passed.

At the next feeding Niki handled the babies with the greatest care. It was easily done. That night he slept in the bed-hammock on the porch with the alarm clock set to ring in two hours.

Twelve o'clock and black darkness; two o'clock, starlight; four o'clock, another dawn about to break; a brighter one, like his future.

Mr. Barnard joined him for the six o'clock feeding.

"You're all right, Niki. You do it like a trained nurse!" he said. "I'll take over on alternate nights so you can get your sleep."

"I want to do it. I go to sleep again fast. Won't you let me, until I'm tired anyway?"

"I'll see. In a few days it will be every three hours, then every four as they get so they can take more nourishment. We'll vary the diet a little perhaps, with diluted evaporated milk, or Pablum. Well, I'm going out to see how Hooper's getting along. He's had a hard time of it these past few days."

Niki's mouth suddenly went dry. "Is he . . . is Hooper sick or anything?"

"No, I don't think he's sick, but he hasn't eaten right or acted right. Could be he was nervous, like the young fathers in hospital waiting rooms."

"Gosh," Niki thought, "I hope that's all that's wrong with him." Even caring for the twins couldn't lift the weight of his guilt.

Mrs. Barnard broke in on his troubled thoughts.

"Niki, come here." In her hands she held a wrist watch with a heavy gold bracelet. "You'll need a watch to tell you when it's feeding time. This was Lewis's. I want you to have it." Courage and kindness shone in her eyes.

Niki stammered his thanks as he carefully stretched the bracelet over his brown hand. He had succeeded in what he had wanted to do. He had made her like him. In a way he had taken Lewis's place; he

had Lewis's watch for his own. It was a challenge to
him to prove worthy of her trust. And he would be
worthy. He'd make her and Mr. Barnard proud of
him. Filled with a high and noble resolve, he worked
that day as he had never worked before.

It was at seven o'clock in the evening that the
telephone rang. Supper had been late, and they were
still sitting at the table, talking. Mr. Barnard answered it, then turned to Niki.

"It's for you." His eyes twinkled as he lowered
his voice. "It's a girl!"

"What? Who?" Niki asked. But he knew. His
mouth felt dry and his heart began to boom like a big
bass drum.

"Hello," he said.

"Do you know who this is?"

"Yes." He knew, too, that voices came through
the receiver so clearly that everyone in the room
shared the conversation.

"How are you?"

"All right." There was a long silence. "What do
you want?"

"Oh, nothing special. We missed you because you
didn't come to the pond last night. All the others
came when it stopped raining. I was going to ask
you if you wanted to come to our camp for the Fourth
of July. Can you?"

"No."

"Why not?"

"Because I can't." Niki didn't know whether to be glad or sorry. He just hoped she would stop talking before she made things worse.

"You can't talk, can you, but I'm calling from the drug store. I'll ask questions and you answer them. Is that all right?"

"No," said Niki, a hint of desperation in his voice. The lump that always churned in his stomach when he thought of their escapade came into his throat, choking him.

"Why not?"

Niki squirmed. He knew it was coming. And the one word HOOPER would be enough to finish him.

"Look, June, I'm busy. I've got a lot to do. I've got to go now. Goodbye. I'll be seeing you."

"But Niki, wait. I wanted to tell you I haven't told anybody anything."

"Okay. Goodbye." As he replaced the receiver, Mrs. Barnard burst out laughing.

"Niki, forgive me," she said, but if you could see your face! You've got such a gift of gab, but you're practically speechless when you talk to a girl."

He mopped the perspiration from his face, grinning now that it was over.

"I couldn't help overhearing," Mr. Barnard remarked. "If you want to go to camp for the Fourth, go ahead. I'll take over your responsibilities for the day. You're too young to be tied down to twins." He laughed heartily.

Niki couldn't see anything so funny about it.

"Who is the girl, if you'll pardon a woman's insatiable curiosity?" Mrs. Barnard asked.

"June Simmons. She has a brother Joe, who's a friend of mine."

"She must be Nate Simmons' little girl. It doesn't seem as though she is old enough to be calling up boy friends, but I know time flies. They're a nice family, Niki. Why don't you ask Joe and June to come here sometime? They might be interested in seeing the chinchillas."

Niki almost choked on his last mouthful of apple pie.

"Yes, go ahead," Mr. Barnard agreed. "We want you to have friends. We'll get cokes and ice cream for refreshments. Ask them any time."

Niki made no reply.

"Why don't you ask June to come?" Mrs. Barnard persisted.

"Because I don't want to," Niki answered, his face getting red.

"Don't tease him any more," Mr. Barnard said,

and to change the subject, added, "Have you decided what to name your twins?"

"Yes. The boy is going to be Mr. Morgan. The girl I'm naming Nikita, for me."

Mr. Barnard was amused. "Fine!" he said. "You can make their record cards any time. Why not now?"

"All right," said Niki.

Carefully he picked out the letters on the typewriter on Mr. Barnard's desk.

```
CLB Mr. Morgan M B5    CLB Nikita      F B6
dam CLB (Happy) A      dam CLB (Happy) A
sire CLB (Hooper) A    sire CLB (Hooper) A
Litter  1M   1F        Litter  1M   1F
     7/2/55                 7/2/55
```

"How's that?" Niki asked as he showed the cards.

"Fine, boy, fine! We'll make a rancher of you, yet!"

Chapter 9 THE CAMP AT ROBBINS' POND

That Fourth of July was one of the few times Niki was homesick for the city. It was the dullest day he had ever known. He couldn't help thinking of the fun he might have had back in Warren, or at Joe's camp. Joe and June . . . they were often in his thoughts, but thoughts of June brought thoughts of Hooper, who was still not eating right. Niki must look after the twins and save Mr. Barnard that much extra work. It was the least he could do.

More and more he worked in the chinchilla house as the days passed. First, washing and filling water

bottles, then changing and sterilizing the removable
screen floors of the cages and putting in clean litter,
and finally taking charge of the pans of fuller's
earth in which the animals took their daily baths;
each duty was important, the last the best of all. Niki
never tired of watching them roll and tumble about in
the talcum-fine dust, and then shake their lustrous
coats after the dry cleaning.

One morning, as he watched one of the younger
pairs, he noticed they had no tattoo marks on their
ears.

"What about Sukey and Sam, Mr. Barnard? Why
haven't they been tattooed?"

"I usually wait until I have several to do and
then tattoo them all at once."

"You do it yourself?"

"Usually. I have to have a helper." He smiled.
The light in Niki's eyes, the eagerness in his face
could not be denied. Charles Barnard knew that the
"young hellion" he had dreaded would presently be
his assistant in tattooing two chinchillas.

"Couldn't we do Sukey and Sam and my twins?
I'd like to see how you do it."

"Your twins are too young. I always wait until
they are four to six months old and their ears are full
size."

"Oh," said Niki. He put a ton of disappointment into the word.

"I suppose we could do Sukey and Sam. It doesn't take long, and it will be easier with you to help me."

"Does it hurt?"

"No. They seem to have very little sensitivity in their ears. They do object to being held, though."

Niki left Sukey's cage and examined Hooper's ear. Hooper looked more chipper today and nibbled Niki's finger through the wire, much to his delight.

"Then how do you do it?" he asked.

"Hooper was done by the expert who graded him. He used an electric outfit with a needle that pricks the holes. It is inked so that it stains the perforations and makes the letters show."

"Same idea as branding cattle so no one will steal them."

"Yes, and a positive identification for the owner, for his records of breedings or sale."

"Poor little Sukey," said Niki as he filled the last water bottle. "It's lucky you don't know what's going to happen to you tomorrow."

As for Niki, he could hardly wait. Every new thing he learned was a step up the ladder. Up the ladder to his own chinchilla ranch!

In the morning Mr. Barnard set out a box containing a bottle of alcohol, a jar of salve, some absorbent cotton and his own tattooing outfit. It consisted of a clamp-type stamp, or punch, into which the letters signifying the ranch and year, or the numbers zero to nine, could be inserted. He showed Niki how it closed tightly to transfer the desired markings to the chinchilla's ear.

Following instructions, Niki held Sukey's hind legs and tail firmly but gently in one hand, and grasped her around the neck to hold her front paws with his other hand. Mr. Barnard swabbed her left ear with a piece of cotton dampened in the alcohol. Niki held his breath as the clamp bit through the tiny ear. Sukey didn't make a sound.

"Good girl," Niki said, beads of sweat standing on his forehead. "You're a brave one, you are!" Tiny dots of light shone through the ear to outline CLB as Mr. Barnard applied salve to aid the healing.

"Now let's have the other ear," Mr. Barnard said as he inserted Sukey's number, B3, in the punch. The operation was soon completed.

Sam was as obstreperous as Sukey was docile. He struggled and squealed, but Niki's firm hold and Mr. Barnard's skill successfully finished the job.

"Now you really belong to us," Niki told him, replacing him in the cage. "You should be proud to wear CLB in your ear."

Mr. Barnard smiled. "You certainly have a way

with animals," he said as he put the tattoo outfit away in its box.

"Thanks, boss," said Niki. "You know there is nothing I'd rather be doing."

The hot July days fell into a pattern of work and relaxation. One of the boys whom he met at Indian Pond asked Niki to join the Bristol Boys' Baseball Team. As soon as the twins were on their three-hour schedule Niki joined the BBB's, and that kept him busy three evenings a week. The days passed quickly.

One day when he went for his swim, he found Joe there.

"Hi, Niki! Race you!" he called, friendly as ever.

Niki was proud to find his stroke had improved so that he could keep up with Joe. It was good to find him so friendly, too.

"Want to come to camp next weekend? If you can stand that feather-brained sister of mine for two whole days," said Joe.

"Thanks. I'd like to, if I can arrange it with Mr. Barnard."

The novelty of feeding baby chinchillas had worn pretty thin, and Niki was glad to be free of his duties for a while. And Joe's camp and the fourteen-foot catboat were what he wanted to see. Never mind about June.

Mr. Barnard was glad to take over so, on Friday evening, with great anticipation, Niki climbed into the front seat of the car with Joe and Joe's father, a silent, but not unfriendly, man. The back seat was piled high with laundry, roofing paper, paint, and cartons of provisions; the trunk held three cakes of ice.

"We'll have to take the bumps easy tonight, Dad," Joe said. "We're what you might call loaded!"

Niki would never forget that ride through the green, hilly country. But lovely as it was, it was only a prelude to the last three miles, three delightfully dangerous miles, when they left the state highway and turned into a narrow dirt road. There were few houses, one tiny settlement with a store.

"That's our nearest grocery store unless we row across the pond," Joe explained, pointing to the dilapidated building. "It's quite a walk, and when we get here it's usually closed."

It didn't look very busy this Friday night. Cows grazed untethered by the roadside; white-haired, barefooted children stood still and stared; yapping dogs ran around the car, frightening the cows, and daring Mr. Simmons to continue if he could, without running over them.

Cautiously they passed, and cautiously continued. As the road grew steadily narrower, it grew rougher.

The bumps and ridges increased in size and number. At the next sharp turn Joe cried, "Look! There's the pond!"

All the cottages were hidden. Just blue water, blue sky, green trees. Niki felt a thrill of pleasure.

"I suppose it looked the same a hundred years ago, maybe a thousand. It's the nearest to the wilderness I've ever been," he commented.

High in the west was a creamy pink afterglow, faintly reflected in the still water. One little breeze made riffles outside the point of pines that jutted into the water, and blew from there to touch their faces. It was cool, clean-smelling, refreshing. Niki inhaled deeply.

"I'll never be satisfied to stay in the city all summer after seeing this," he exclaimed.

"From here on to our end of the pond, it's our own private way," said Joe as he jumped out to unlock the padlock that fastened a wide white gate. "We keep it locked because the road is too narrow for two cars to pass."

"I shouldn't think many people would ever find their way in here. But you couldn't blame them for trying, if they know what it's like."

The way became narrower, steeper, rockier; the trees came closer; the ruts were deeper, and at times the single track was hidden in deep grass. At other

times they bucked over outcroppings of rock that
made driving an adventure about like putting a car
over a stone wall.

Mr. Simmons ground along in low gear all the
way, easing his car over the bumps. He switched on
the lights, but Joe asked him to turn them off. "Until
we get through the hemlocks, Dad," he said. In a
minute Niki knew why he had asked, for in the semi-
darkness, the whole grove was scintillating with
fireflies.

"Do you like it so far?" Joe asked.

"You bet I do."

When the car lights were on again, they focused
on a steep tunnel through the woods, little wider than
a footpath. Down that, up another abrupt and rocky
turn, and through the trees they saw the pond again.
By the fading light Niki could make out two little
cabins down below at the water's edge. The road
ended in a small clearing.

"Hi, Niki!" June called, running to meet them.
With her was a friend, Patty Nickerson, whom Niki
had met at Indian Pond. Patty was quiet, plain; she
couldn't compare with June, but Niki liked her. In
fact, at that moment he liked everything and everybody.

"Hi, kids," he sang out. "It's a wonderful place
you've got here."

"Wait till you see the gorge and Piney Point and Devil's Rocks. We're going to show you all over the place tomorrow," June answered.

Loaded with bags and groceries, they made their way into the cabin, crossed the porch and the living room, and entered the kitchen.

"Mom, where are you?" June called as they dumped their bundles on the kitchen shelf. "Oh, I see her at the well. Mom! Here's Niki!"

Mom was a plump little woman, with yellow hair like June's, brown eyes like June's, and a warm smile of welcome. Niki liked her immediately.

"How do you do, Niki," she said, "we're glad you could come."

"So am I, Mrs. Simmons. I've read about places like this, but I've never seen one before. I felt like a pioneer coming in through the forest — Lewis and Clark, or Henry Hudson, or somebody. It's a grand place. May I help you with that?" He took the pail of water and carried it to its place beside the kitchen sink.

"What a nice boy you are!" she said. Niki pushed up the wave in his hair and gave her his most charming smile. He was sure she liked him, but he had his doubts about June's father.

"Here comes Dad with the ice. Help me get things out of the top of the ice box."

From then on every minute was full. Niki met June's aunt and uncle, who were weekend guests, and the Bensons who lived in the other cabin, all jolly, friendly people. He inspected the tent where he and Joe were to sleep under the pines at the water's edge. They all had a bite to eat, and what a bite it was! It was all informal and homey, and Niki was interested in everything from the well and the kerosene lamps to Joe's catboat and the roofing job.

Bright lights shone from across the pond where crowds were enjoying the public beach attractions.

"Let's go to the pavilion tonight. I want to dance," insisted June.

Arguments followed, but as usual June won out. They rowed across the pond, beached the skiff, and with lights and music and gayety entered a different world. Niki danced with June several times, then with Patty. When he looked for June again, he experienced the same uncomfortable feeling that had kept him awake most of one restless night, for June was dancing with Toby.

Niki walked down to the shore. The hall had become noisy and stuffy. Outdoors was better where a golden moon shone in the sky. It had never looked so bright or big before. Niki looked for the Simmons camp, but it was hidden among the trees. Someday, he resolved. he would have a camp like that, way off in the woods, and a sailboat, too, and his own rowboat, and his own stretch of private, sandy beach; someday when his chinchilla ranch had made him a rich man. He would make trips to the city, mostly to New York, but he would live on his ranch, and spend the weekends at a camp like the Simmons.'

The music stopped so he went in to find June.

"Hello, Toby, imagine seeing you here," he said patronizingly to the big fellow as June greeted him with a smile.

"That goes double for you," Toby answered. "Okay, June, just remember what I told you."

After he had left them, Niki asked June what he meant.

"Oh, nothing, only he doesn't like your being here at our camp. But what do we care?"

"Poor old Toby! It's just too bad about him!" Nothing could dim Niki's happiness. Not tonight, anyway.

Back at camp came another new experience: sleeping out of doors. A cool breeze blew the mosquitoes away, so Niki and Joe took their blankets out onto the pine needles. Niki was tired. It was his first night of uninterrupted sleep since he had had the baby chinchillas to feed, and how he slept!

When he awoke it was broad daylight. Joe was gone. Niki barely had time for a morning dip before the welcome call of "Come and get it," accompanied by the noisy ringing of a cowbell, brought people hurrying from all directions.

Nothing had ever tasted so good as those meals at camp, served outdoors on a long, bare table. No hours ever passed so quickly as did the hours that weekend. Sailing, swimming, exploring, taking pictures, practicing archery, at which Joe and June were experts, and eating, at which they were all experts; helping Mr. Simmons lay roofing paper — everything was fun. Before they could believe it, Saturday was gone, and Sunday, too.

Late in the evening they rowed across the pond in the moonlight, Niki at the oars, pulling with a strong, even stroke. He wished it were Friday again, with the weekend beginning instead of ending. All too soon Joe said, "It's time we were heading back. Everybody has to get off early tomorrow morning and Dad wants us in by eleven."

"I suppose," Niki agreed, heading for the shore. Before it touched the sand, Joe sprang lightly from the bow to pull the boat in. He carefully fastened the rope to an eyebolt set in a rock. Patty followed him ashore.

"Come on, you two," he called. "Let's go up to the house and see if there's anything left to eat before we turn in."

"Niki, I want to sit here a minute," June coaxed. "You don't want to go in, do you?"

"Okay by me," Niki said.

The boat drifted a little way out, then swung in towards shore. The only sound was the soft lapping of water against its sides.

"Did Mr. Barnard ever find out about our going to see the chinchillas?" she asked.

"No."

"Is the one that got away all right?"

"I think so. He had me scared because he didn't eat for a few days, but I think he's all right now. Have you told anybody?"

"Oh, no! I wouldn't want you to lose your job and have to go away from Bristol." She looked awfully pretty with the moonlight shining on her yellow hair.

"Don't worry; I'm in right with the Barnards. Say, I haven't told you about my twins!" With gusto and in great detail, he told her the story.

"Did you name them for me and Joe?"

"I wanted to name the girl for you, June, but I knew the Barnards would kid me, so I named her Nikita, for me. The other one I named Mr. Morgan for the principal of the high school in Warren. I told you about him. He got me this job, and he's a prince if there ever was one."

Niki reached forward and took June's hands in his.

"Sure and you're lovely, lovely as the moonlight," he said, his heart thumping wildly against his ribs, his hands trembling as he felt her fingers tighten their pressure.

Her voice was cool and steady as she asked him more questions about Mr. Morgan and the chinchillas. "How many have you at home where you live?" she wanted to know.

For a long moment Niki was silent. Then, moved by an emotion he could not explain, he answered her. "June," he said, his dark eyes holding hers, "I didn't tell you the truth that day at Table Rock. I, well, I wanted you to like me, and I guess I wanted to sound important or something."

"I do like you," she said, freeing one hand and trailing her fingers in the water.

Her words gave him the courage to go on.

"I haven't any chinchillas," he confessed. "In fact, I had never seen one until I came to Mr. Barnard's. I was sent here because I got into trouble in Warren. I was with some boys when they stole a car and smashed it up. Mr. Morgan sent me here. It was my last chance to make good." The words came hard, but he spoke them. "It was this or reform school. But I'm making good now."

She looked down to see the drops she shook from her fingers glisten in the moonlight, then gave him both her hands again. As their eyes met, she squeezed his fingers hard.

"I'm glad you told me," she said.

"And you still like me, a little bit?" he pleaded.

"Of course I do."

"Hey, what goes on here?" a loud, angry voice interrupted, accompanied by a crashing in the under-brush. Niki turned to see June's father hauling in the skiff.

"June, go up to the house. It's nearly twelve o'clock."

"But, Daddy, it can't be. We were just talking a minute. Niki was telling me about his chinchillas."

"You've had two days to talk. Go on. I mean it. No fooling." His face was contorted with anger as he spat out the words.

"Gee, I'm sorry, Mr. Simmons," Niki said in apology. "I had no idea it was that late."

Mr. Simmons ignored him. He started up the path with June.

"You were hiding in the bushes to spy on us. My own father. I'm so ashamed I could die, knowing that you'd do a thing like that," and June began to cry.

"I was not spying on you. I told you to get in by

eleven, because people want to get some sleep. Why couldn't you come when Joe did?"

"Because I wanted to talk to Niki. He's the nicest boy I've ever known, and now you've humiliated me in front of him, and I'll never, never get over it."

"There's nothing to get humiliated over and you know it. Now for Heaven's sake be quiet."

The voices ceased. Niki scowled. How much had Mr. Simmons overheard? Well, what he had told about himself was the truth. Mr. Simmons would have had to find it out sometime. And Hooper was all right again, so that didn't matter so much either. He decided it was not worth worrying about as he rolled up in his blanket beside Joe and went to sleep.

Chapter 10 **UNWELCOME VISITORS**

In the morning Niki left early with Mr. Simmons. After a few unsuccessful attempts at conversation, he stopped trying and they rode in silence to the center of Bristol.

"Do you mind walking from here?" Mr. Simmons asked.

"No. That's all right. Thank you, sir, for a nice weekend."

Mr. Simmons loosened up a little. "I'm glad you enjoyed it. Come again sometime."

Boy! That was nice of him! Niki's heart suddenly warmed towards the man. Of course he had to be careful with a daughter like June. Careful about who came to visit them, and how late she stayed out nights with a boy. But he said "Come again sometime." Niki whistled all the way up the hill.

The Barnards were in the kitchen when he arrived home.

"Good morning to the both of you. Say, I had a swell time. They've got a beautiful place there." Niki told them all about it. "How's everything around here? Did my twins miss me?"

"Your twins are all right. But Hooper isn't."

"What's the matter?"

"I don't know what happened. You remember he didn't act right or eat right a couple of weeks back, then he seemed to get over it. But these last few days I've been worried. I called the vet Saturday and he thinks Hooper was injured on his face and probably internally. He took him to his hospital, but there was nothing he could do except put him to sleep, out of his misery. I was just telling Martha I'd rather it had been any one of the others. But Hooper was my best male. Not only that, he was such a friendly little thing. I'd give a lot to know what happened to him."

Funny how, in an instant, the light could go out

and everything inside you be darkness. Niki felt as though some huge, cruel hand had squeezed the breath out of his body.

"It's too bad," he said. His mouth was dry; he felt sick all over. Hooper had suffered and lost his life because he, Niki, was a coward. The boy was glad to get away to his own room. Oh, if he had only told Mr. Barnard the whole story. There was no use telling now. There was only one way to make amends. He must work as he had never worked before. Morning, noon, and night he must work. And someday he must come back to Bristol and make Mr. Barnard a present of the champion blue of the whole world. But even that wouldn't be Hooper.

Niki did work during the weeks that followed. He read everything he could find about chinchillas and had long talks with Mr. Barnard about kinds of equipment, grading standards, breeding, heredity, and treatment of disease. He helped daily, cleaning cages, preparing meals. All this in addition to the tasks he had done before.

When Nikita and Mr. Morgan were transferred to the building and a cage of their own, it was a proud day for Niki because Mr. Barnard said to him, "Any time you want to go out there and play with your pets, go ahead. I know I can trust you not to interfere with the other animals."

Niki made the most of the privilege. The twins were healthy and growing fast. Because they were accustomed to his handling them, Niki could let them run up his sleeve, cuddle under his chin, and nibble his ear. Mr. Morgan, like Hooper, showed definitely blue shading; Nikita, though lighter, was a beauty, too.

On the twenty-third of July another baby was born. This time Chica and Ande were the proud parents. Niki had a chance to see what normal chinchilla mother and father love was like. There never was a happier family. Ande would rub his nose against Chica's face and tell her how wonderful she was. He took his turn caring for the baby while Chica ate her meals. When the baby was in the hollow log, Ande sat at one end, on guard.

"I wonder why Happy acted the way she did when her twins were born," Niki said to Mr. Barnard after watching Chica's motherliness.

"She was only eleven months old, which is a bit young," Mr. Barnard explained. "Then she turned against Hooper, which is most unusual. Almost always pairs are especially devoted as the time draws near for the young to be born, but Happy was always skittish and temperamental."

"Still I can't see why she would abuse her babies.

She went after Nikita as though she wanted to kill her."

"Perhaps that baby hurt her when it nursed. They are born with teeth, you know, and that sometimes happens. They are fine babies, though. A great credit to their godfather, if that's what you are."

"Are you going to find a new mate for Happy?" Niki's thoughts were full of Hooper as he asked. He couldn't take credit for anything. Hooper's death, and very likely Happy's queer behavior too, were his fault.

Mr. Barnard interrupted the gloomy thoughts. "I'm going to put Blue Boy in with her and see how he makes out. This new female of Chica's we can mate with your male when they're old enough."

"What about Nikita?"

"We'll find a mate for her. If a couple get used to each other when they're young, they often live happily ever after. Many mate for life, but a female can kill a male in about two seconds if she is suddenly confronted with one she doesn't like. I've had that happen just once."

"I learn more from talking to you five minutes than from all the articles in the magazines."

"I'm glad to help you, Niki, for there is a great future in this business for anybody who is really interested. I know you are. And you're starting right."

Niki went for his afternoon swim with a lighter heart than he had had since Hooper's death. He missed June and Joe. Toby he never saw. But the rest of the crowd were friends, now, and the sunny hours at the pond passed quickly and pleasantly.

A few nights later the Barnards came home from the Post Office to find Niki in the dining room, the table strewn with pictures.

"I've finally got all my prints together," he explained. "You haven't seen these last ones I took at camp. I've got a set for my mother, and some for Mr. Morgan and Jokey, and some for Joe and June. I'm writing the titles on the back. Then I'm going to write to my mother and explain her set."

"Wouldn't you like to ask her to visit you before the summer is over?" Mrs. Barnard asked.

"You bet I would." Niki's eyes shone as he thought about it. "She'd love it. She's always wanted to live in the country again. When do you want her to come?"

"Why not ask her for the week before Labor Day? Then you can go back together."

"That's great. Thanks. She can plan her vacation for that week. These pictures took a big hunk out of

my surplus cash, but from now on I'm going to save
my money so I can send her a bank check for her
railroad ticket. It will come just right, for her birthday is August 27th, and it will be the best present
I've ever been able to give her. You know you're a
couple of swell folks? Have you got a big envelope?
I want to write that letter!"

Mr. Barnard opened his desk and gave Niki an
envelope.

"Thanks." Niki pointed to the pictures the Barnards were looking at. "She'll show those to the
people at the office and all the family and the neighbors. You know it meant a lot to her that I could be
here this summer."

Up the stairs he went, two at a time. He hadn't
thought much about his mother for the days had
been so full, but now it seemed as though he could
hardly wait to have her meet the Barnards, and
Herky, and the chinchillas.

He looked at the calendar. It didn't seem possible
that the summer was half gone. He thought back to
his city home. It was a funny thing. He would never
have believed it a month ago, but he didn't want to
go back. He sighed and began his letter. It turned out
to be a long one. It was nearly finished when he
heard Hercules barking and Mr. Barnard greeting
someone at the door.

"Come in. Glad to see you."

Voices could be heard indistinctly. Probably neighbors whom Niki did not know. He went on with his letter. "You'll see a big difference in me," he wrote. "I haven't gained weight, but my muscles are like iron, and I'm the color of an Indian, only blacker. I work hard for the Barnards, but it's all right. I'm glad to. They have been very good to me and they deserve the best of everything."

Just then Mr. Barnard called, "Niki, I want you."

"Okay. I'll be there in a minute."

It was quite a feat to go down the stairs two at a time, but Niki managed to do it without breaking his neck.

"Yes, sir, here I am," he said triumphantly as he reached the hall.

He stopped in the doorway and the smile left his face. For Mr. Simmons was standing there, and June. When she saw Niki she flung herself into Mrs. Barnard's arms and burst out crying. The two men's faces were stern and angry.

Mr. Barnard spoke first. "Well, Niki, this looks like the end."

Niki's face was white, his eyes staring at first one person, then another.

"June's been telling us about her visit to the chinchillas."

Niki swallowed the lump in his throat. It seemed as though deep inside his heart, he had always known this would happen. It was like a repeat performance of something he had lived through before.

"Yes, sir," he said.

Then June's father took over, his lips trembling as he tried to keep his self-control. "You made her promise not to tell. And she wouldn't have, I suppose, if it hadn't led to other things. But I got it out of her at last. The whole story."

"Yes, sir." Niki didn't know what the man was talking about. It felt now like a bad dream. He hoped it would end soon so he could go back and finish his letter. The pressure inside his head made him feel dizzy.

"You and your friend Toby." The scorn in Mr. Simmons' voice cut through to Niki's consciousness.

"Toby isn't my friend." Even if it was a dream, he wouldn't have Toby for a friend.

"Well, you're two of a kind. Did you know he has been blackmailing June ever since he learned about this business? And she's been lying to me and going on dates with him. Why? Just to protect you, you contemptible sneak."

"I'm sorry." That wasn't the thing to say, but if June had told Toby, nothing mattered anyway. And with Mr. Barnard looking at him with cold, unfriendly eyes Niki couldn't think straight.

"You're sorry!" Mr. Simmons clenched his fists and beat them together. "Is that all you can say? Mr. Barnard trusting you, and you sneaking in behind his back and letting the chinchillas out of their cages. If there is any shred of manliness in you, say something."

Only silence in the room, broken by June's quiet sobbing. Niki wished the horrible buzzing in his ears would stop. He looked again at Mr. Barnard. His face looked old and drawn. He looked at Mrs. Barnard as she softly patted June's hair. When she lifted her eyes and met his appealing gaze, she turned her face away, her lips one thin, straight line.

It was Mr. Simmons, the silent man, who did all the talking. "You frightened her with all the talk about everything being her fault because she dropped the chinchilla, and telling her that Mr. Barnard could bring suit against us. As if you didn't know you alone were to blame for going in there and opening that cage. You deserve a good thrashing if ever a boy did." His face, red as fire, seemed to swell larger and larger and larger.

Mr. Barnard raised his head slowly as if to speak, but Mr. Simmons stopped him. "You should never have taken a boy like this and turned him loose with a fine crowd of young folks. A boy who is a thief."

"That's not true." Niki's eyes blazed as he answered.

"I've found out all about you and that gang in Warren. I know why you're here. You were always in trouble, breaking windows, snatching bags, holding up a candy store and other —"

"Not me," Niki shouted at him. "I wasn't in on any stealing."

"Weren't you with a gang that stole a car and smashed it up? Weren't you? Can you deny that?"

Niki tried to speak, but no words came. This was it. The end. The end of trying. The end of everything. Then why didn't it end? Why did they still stand there? Why didn't they go home?

Mr. Barnard was talking. The words came from a great distance, from miles away. "I know his history. He has many good qualities, but a weak link somewhere. He lacks courage to do the hard thing. It was easier to stick with the gang than to break away, even though he knew it would end in trouble. When they stole the car it was easier to lie than to speak the truth, so he lied."

Niki bent his head. The awful night was with him again. He could bear no more. He turned to leave the room when Mr. Barnard stopped him. "As to your going to the chinchilla house, that I could forgive, and did forgive. But to let an animal suffer day after day from injuries you caused and must have suspected, and not be man enough to own up to the wrong you'd done, that I cannot and will not forgive. Go to your room and pack your bag. Be ready to leave on the early train."

He stopped speaking. June's father touched her shoulder.

"Come on. We're going home."

Niki caught one glimpse of her swollen, tear-stained face as they went to the door with Mr. Barnard. June didn't speak. Neither did Niki.

He stumbled up the stairs to his room. The letter to his mother was still on the table. Slowly he tore it into bits and dropped the pieces into the waste basket.

Chapter 11 **NIGHT OF DECISION**

For a long time Niki sat staring out the window at the dark night. His head ached terribly. His thoughts circled endlessly. From them questions shot off like comets. Why had June told Toby everything? Why had she told her father? He had been too confused to wonder before.

"A good thrashing!" How easy that kind of punishment was. It hurt, and then it was over. But this he would remember all his life, like the other night that was indelibly etched in his memory, when brakes screamed, and the police came, and the questions,

questions, questions. He had wanted to tell the truth. But it was true, what Mr. Barnard said. He was afraid when things were hard to do. He took the easier way whenever he could, even if he knew it was wrong.

He dragged his thoughts back to the present. What should he do now? Go home? He couldn't do that. He couldn't face Mr. Morgan and his mother and his grandmother. He could go away somewhere. He still had five dollars, a little more, enough to keep him till he got a job. He could pass for sixteen easy. He could hitchhike, the farther west the better, earning enough money day by day to keep him going.

He decided to do it, and felt better after making the decision. He wouldn't stay here where everyone was against him. No. Not even if they asked him. Quickly he changed his clothes and packed his bag. Without a glance he dropped his father's picture in it. He would leave tonight and be far away before the Barnards missed him. And in the west he would find work and make a new life for himself.

It was quarter of eleven by his wrist watch. Should he take it with him? Well, why not? He would need it. It was his. He tried to think of Mrs. Barnard, not as she looked when she gave it to him, but as she had looked tonight when he turned to her for help and her mouth was a thin, straight line. Even she had failed him.

Quietly he tiptoed down the stairs. The living room door was open. Mr. Barnard sat beside the table, his head resting on his hand as he looked at the pictures Niki had left there. He turned some over to read the words on the back. Niki's throat tightened as he remembered them. "Our chinchillas," "Mother Barnard," "My pal Herky," My good friend, Mr. B."

Niki dared not move. For a long time he stood there watching, thinking. Mr. Barnard liked him . . . in a way, he had taken Lewis's place. He had to face it. They had been good to him. It was he who had failed. And what was he doing now? Running away. Wasn't that the same thing right over again? Wasn't running away instead of facing this trouble and taking the consequences the weak link breaking again?

Was he really a coward? What was the right thing to do? Not the easiest thing, but the right thing? Noiselessly he crept back up the stairs.

He knelt by the open window to think it out. Never had he tried so hard to see himself honestly, balancing his good points against the weak ones. At last he heard Mr. Barnard go to his room. Then, all was quiet. It was time to leave if he was going . . . but was he absolutely sure he wanted to?

At last he reached his decision. He would not run away. He would face the consequences. He undressed, crawled into bed, and exhausted, slept.

In the morning he wore his good clothes to breakfast. His face was set and there were dark circles under his eyes. It was a silent meal.

As they rose from the table he said, "Mr. Barnard, I've got to talk to you."

"What more is there to say?"

"Last night I made up my mind to run away. When I came downstairs at eleven o'clock you were still in the living room, so I had to go back and think some more. And it came clear at last that running away was that weak link breaking again. I don't want to be a weak character. I want to be a real man, like you."

Niki's voice played tricks on him, but he went on. "I promised Mr. Morgan I would stick it out no matter what happened, that I wouldn't quit or get thrown out. I wish you'd give me one more chance so I can keep my promise."

"You've forfeited your right to ask." Mr. Barnard's voice was cold, but there was sadness in his eyes.

"I know it. It's just that you're the one man in a thousand who might give a fellow one more last chance."

For a long time Mr. Barnard looked at Niki. Then slowly he shook his head. What a boy he was! He certainly could twist the facts to his own advantage.

Seeing him hesitate, Niki went on, "About Hooper. I tried to tell you. Honestly I did. But at first I was afraid, and I couldn't get the words out. After that I thought he was moping because Happy didn't like him any more, and after that I thought he was going to be all right again. I feel awful to think of Hooper suffering."

"So do I. This whole thing has hit me pretty hard."

"Please give me one more chance." Tears welled up in Niki's eyes. Mr. Barnard could not doubt his sincerity.

"Go to your room. I'll let you know."

Niki waited there. The minutes seemed like hours. He couldn't stand it, just sitting there. He dressed in his working clothes to go to the barn.

Mr. Barnard, still in the kitchen, looked up in surprise.

"I'll get the cows and milk them," Niki explained, before Mr. Barnard could object. "I haven't unpacked my bag."

Niki milked, easily, quickly. Then down the green lane he made his way, listening to the bobwhite's call and whistling his answer. Would this be his last time? Never before had he been so conscious of the sweetness of a summer morning.

"Oh, God," he whispered as he lifted the pasture

bars into place, "please make him give me one more chance. Just this once."

Niki finished the barn chores and returned to the kitchen, surprised to find Mr. Barnard still in the house.

"The milk is in the cooler," he said, "and I've cleaned out the stalls and fed the hens." Then he stood there, not knowing what to do next.

Mr. Barnard spoke without looking at the boy.

"We've reached our decision about what to do with you. I've had a talk with Mr. Morgan. You are to stay here, not because I want you, or because you deserve it, but because sending you back in disgrace would probably destroy the few good qualities you have, and break your mother's heart. So you are getting the chance you asked for."

"You'll never be sorry, Mr. Barnard, I promise you that."

"Your promises come too easily. They aren't worth much."

The boy's face flushed, but he did not speak. He watched as Mr. Barnard took the key to the chinchilla house from the hook where it had always hung and attached it to his key ring.

"You must realize that having you here has been a costly experiment," he said coldly.

No punishment could have hurt Niki more. But he

was staying. He would face the consequences as he had determined to do.

From then on his relationship with the Barnards was changed. It didn't show much on the surface, but the old free and easy friendliness was gone. It was as though an invisible wall lay between them beyond which Niki could not pass — a wall of distrust of Niki's own building. Mr. Barnard seldom mentioned the chinchillas. Although Niki often wondered about Mr. Morgan and Nikita, and how they were growing, and if they would remember him, he asked no questions.

The hot days of early August passed. There was always plenty of work to be done. Niki kept at it with desperate faithfulness, trying to win back what he had destroyed.

One afternoon when he was at home alone, the postman left a small package addressed to Mr. Barnard and asked Niki to sign for it. He wondered what could be inside, for it felt like an empty box, although it was insured. Curious, he shook it. Nothing rattled.

As he passed it to Mr. Barnard, he remarked, "It feels like nothing at all."

"Open it. You'll see."

Niki cut the string and lifted the cover. Filled with curiosity he removed the tissue paper wrappings.

"Oh no!" he exclaimed when he saw what it was, pushing the box away.

Mr. Barnard lifted out a soft, shimmering blue-gray pelt.

"It's all that's left of Hooper, Niki."

About the size of a man's hand, light as a feather, soft as the air, still showing the shape of the little head, this supple bit of fur had once been Hooper. Mr. Barnard examined the identification tag which was clipped through the stiff ear. He tossed the pelt to Niki.

"You can have it. Call it your summer's pay." Mr. Barnard's voice was harsh with bitterness. "I wouldn't have taken a thousand dollars for it once."

"Charles, don't talk like that, please," his wife implored.

"I'm sorry, Martha." He put the skin back in the box and threw it into a desk drawer, closed the drawer, and quickly left the room.

A long, quivering sigh of remorse broke from Niki.

"Can't I ever get away from it?" he asked. His shoulders slumped as he bent over the table, his head on his hand, his long fingers tunneling back and forth through the dark waves of his hair.

Mrs. Barnard touched his shoulder gently. "Niki,

if remembering helps you to have the courage to do the right thing next time, Hooper won't have died in vain. That sounds funny, I know, to talk about an animal like that. But I do know how hard you're trying to make up for the wrong you did. Charles knows it, too. He is very fond of you, Niki. More than you know. That's why it hurts him so much."

Niki looked into her kind blue eyes.

"I'll never forget Hooper," he said. "Not if I live to be a hundred. And I've learned a lot of things this summer. There're some mistakes I'll never make again."

"I'm sure of that. You know, I've been thinking about your mother. I'd still like to have her visit us if you care to ask her."

"Thanks, but I don't want to ask her now." He had never told his mother about Hooper, and from her letters he was sure Mr. Morgan had not talked to her. He couldn't bear to have her know why he no longer had access to the chinchillas, not even his twins. He sighed again as he thought of the eager letter he had written the night of the Simmons' visit, and the questions that had remained unanswered ever since.

But Mrs. Barnard insisted. "Niki, I want you to ask her. I want to meet her. And you say she loves the country. Write to her today. The summer's going fast."

"All right. I'll ask her." Niki wrote the invitation, but it was very different from the earlier one which he had destroyed.

Chapter 12   AN OLD FRIEND FINDS NIKI

Even the nights were hot that August. Very often
Niki came downstairs to sleep on the screened porch,
with Hercules for company. He listened to the night
sounds, the crickets' rapid chirping, the repeated
call of the whippoorwill, the whimpering cry of
screech owls. He watched the changing colors of
those summer nights, sharply etched in black and
white when the moon shone, or dimly seen when dampness rose from the pond like river smoke. With the
dawn came the twittering of awakening birds and the

138

hoarse cawing of a dozen crows. Often they were restless nights, but Niki loved them.

The days were busy with chores indoors and out. When it was too hot for cultivating, he helped at odd jobs, sharpening tools, filing a saw, whitewashing the barn. Usually from noon until five he was free to go swimming. They were good days. They passed quickly.

One evening while Niki was watering the lawn, Charles Barnard joined him. "Never mind about the grass," he said. "Give the flowers a good soaking. I want to save Martha's garden, but I'm worried about our water. I've never seen the well as low as it is now."

Niki realized the situation must be serious, because Mr. Barnard was proud of his beautiful lawn. Niki watched him as he pulled up a stake that had been set for his wife's tall dahlias. The soil was dry all the way down; the stake came up clean and easy.

"I don't like it," Mr. Barnard said, shaking his head. "And the weather forecast says no rain in sight. We've got to have more water." He replaced the stake slowly. "I hate to spend the money, but I can't go through this every August. I'm going over to see Sam Bumpus right away. This afternoon."

"Does he dig wells?" Niki asked. He liked Sam

Bumpus, and it would be interesting to see how well-digging was done.

"He doesn't dig them. Sam's a water dowser."

A water dowser. Somewhere in the back of Niki's mind the meaning of those words was stored away. He wrinkled his forehead, trying to remember. It was his science teacher — yes, his science teacher had told the class about it: a man, holding a forked stick, called a divining rod, walked around with it, asking it questions, and it pointed to water. There were books about it at the library, he had said, and Niki had always meant to read them, but he had never done it. The whole business had sounded fishy to him, he remembered, and the teacher had ridiculed it as unscientific.

"Do you believe in that stuff?" he asked, studying Mr. Barnard's face.

"Yes. I don't pretend to understand it, but I know Sam has located water on many farms around here. I've seen him do it."

Niki kept thinking about it. To have seen a water-dowser at work would be something to talk about when he went back to Warren High. And he'd make a good story of it to tell his grandmother, to match her tales of leprechauns and banshees.

Immediately after lunch the Barnards got ready

to go to Sam's place. Mrs. Barnard smiled at Niki as
he held the door open for her to get into the car.

"I suppose if Sam finds water, Charles will get
his irrigating system. Then he'll want to set out his
thousand yews and white pine seedlings, and he'll
work all the time and never take me to ride."

"Don't forget the junipers," Mr. Barnard said,
laughing.

He must like to hoe better than I do, Niki thought,
as they drove away, and he started for the pond.

Soon he was racing a couple of boys to Table
Rock and back, not to win, but for the satisfaction
of measuring his improvement. As he walked ashore,
he noticed a fellow leaning against a pine tree. Niki
stopped and stared. There was something awfully
familiar about the pink shirt and faded dungarees.

"Jokey Perry!" he yelled. "Where on earth did
you come from?"

"Hiya, Niki," Jokey called back. "Is this the way
you work on a farm?"

Niki grinned as he stepped onto the hot sand, his
strong brown body gleaming wet in the sun. He
doubled his fist and flexed his muscles.

"See that?" he asked. "Sure, I work. Plenty. But
when it's as hot as this I get time off for swimming.
I live right up there on the hill."

"Yeah, I know. The fellow at the gasoline station told me. He said I'd probably find you here." For
a moment Jokey's eyes met Niki's fair and square,
then slid off to glance uneasily around the pond.

"How did you get here?"

"Come out to the road. I'll show you."

While Niki toweled himself and put on his
clothes, he experienced feelings he could not explain. Not that he wasn't glad to see his old pal, but
it seemed as though Jokey belonged to a different
world, and that with his coming, its troubles were
returning.

"You with somebody?" he asked.

"No. I've got my own car. It's over there."

"What do you mean, it's yours?" A dozen questions flashed through Niki's mind. Jokey wouldn't be
sixteen until October. How could he have a license
and own a car? If he had a car, why wasn't he on top
of the world, shouting about it, instead of being so
quiet? And a car belonging to Jokey should have
been a sporty buggy, bright orange or flaming red instead of the neat black Chevrolet sedan, perhaps
ten years old, that was parked beside the road.

But it was Jokey's all right, for his voice was
proud as he said, "Get in. I'll give you a ride." Niki
got in. Jokey stepped on the starter and the motor
purred. "Isn't that sweet?" he asked. "She's got

power, too." He proved it as they turned from Indian Pond Road onto the state highway. Forty, fifty, sixty, easy and smooth, then back to a safe forty while he told about it.

The car was his creation. He had bought it for twenty-five bucks, and with the help of one of the garage mechanics, a young fellow named Arthur, he had stripped it to the chassis and reassembled it with new fenders, radiator grill, and other parts picked up on used car lots. Then he had given it the paint job. The motor, too, was his baby. He had worked over it for weeks in his spare time to get it perfect.

Niki listened with growing respect for his old pal.

"Want to drive?" Jokey asked.

"Sure," Niki answered. He knew how to shift gears and steer because he had driven other fellows' cars back and forth around the filling station when Deego worked there.

He walked around the car and got into the driver's seat, made the shifts quietly, and felt the surge of power as his foot pressed the accelerator. He grinned with happiness and kept a steady hand on the wheel. There was little traffic, but he took it easy, grateful for Jokey's confidence in him, and determined to prove he could drive carefully and observe all traffic laws.

Good old Jokey! If he could make this wonderful

jalopy out of old cars, he could build others for his friends. It brought Niki's dream of owning one from the distant future to the present, practically. He'd be sixteen in December. It would take money — twenty-five dollars — but he could earn that much before his birthday.

"You're doing fine," Jokey told him. "Keep her under forty."

"Sure." Obediently Niki lifted his toe and watched the sensitive needle swing back to thirty-five. "This is a good cruising speed," he said. "How is she on gas?" The gas gauge needle, he noticed, was swinging over Empty.

"I meant to get some. Turn back at the next cross-over. Take it easy. Give your left turn signal."

Niki did all those things, but as he started to swing, a horn blared in his ear and a car shot by on his left, missing them by inches.

"Wow! Where did he come from?" Niki asked, a cold shiver running down his back and making his foot tremble on the brake pedal.

"You didn't look in your mirror. Shove over and let me drive. We can't afford to have accidents."

Niki shoved over without a word, while Jokey was getting out and coming around to the other side to take the wheel again. In spite of his trying to be so careful, Niki thought, that could have been it! He watched every move as Jokey drove, determined to become as good a driver as his friend was. At the filling station he paid for the dollar's worth of gas that Jokey ordered, and finding another half dollar in his jeans, treated to cokes and hot dogs from the lunch bar.

As they sat in the car eating, Jokey said suddenly, "How would you like to go to Denver with me?"

"Denver, Colorado?" Niki asked, unbelieving. "Spill it, Jokey, tell me all."

Jokey pulled a letter from his pocket. "My father's in Denver," he said.

"Oh, he is?" Niki knew how Jokey felt about his father.

All the happy memories the boy had were centered around his dad, for his mother had died when Jokey was a baby. It was his father who had played with him and read him stories, and as he grew older, had taken him to the zoo, and to ball games, and had let him take their old car apart and put it together again. For a while they kept their home, but when the older sisters married, Jokey and his father had taken a room in the grandparents' flat.

Then came the Korean War, and Jokey's father had re-enlisted in the Navy. Every morning Jokey had gone to church to say a prayer for his father's safety. Sometimes Niki had gone with him, filled with awe

at the change in Jokey as he reverently lit a candle
and said a prayer.

When the war was over, his father had come
back safe and sound, but restless, and the next year
he had left again to go west. He paid Jokey's board
regularly, and wrote occasionally. About a year ago,
Niki knew, he had married. But Jokey stayed on
with the old folks.

It was Mr. Morgan who insisted that Jokey
write to his father and tell him about the trouble he
had gotten into with Deego's gang, and this long letter
from Denver was the answer.

"He says he's got a good job now, foreman in
a big garage, and when I finish school he wants me
to go out there and live with them. Gee, Niki," Jokey's voice grew husky, "I'd love to see my dad." He
reached into the glove compartment and took out a
map. "I can't wait to finish school. I'm going now."

"You mean you want me to go with you and live
in Denver?" Niki asked. "I'd like to, Jokey, but I
don't know anything about fixing cars, and anyway,
I can't leave the Barnards."

Jokey's face fell. "I thought you were my pal.
When we used to talk about going west, you were
crazy to go. And this isn't foolish kid stuff like going
to see Indians and cowboys. We're going to work.
We'll have real jobs. On weekends and our days

off, we can drive all around, up the mountains and everywhere. There are uranium deposits in Colorado. We might discover a mine. Plenty of people have."

"I'd like to go all right," Niki repeated. For a minute he let his thoughts travel along broad highways to the west. The West! A magic word, conjuring up all the things a boy's heart could wish for. And what an adventurous way to go, he and Jokey, on their own, crossing the desert, camping out, cooking meals beside some vast, yawning canyon, curling up in blankets to sleep in sight of towering mountains capped with glaciers and never-melting snow.

"My father will find a job for you," Jokey promised. "You can wash cars and sell gas part time while you're learning repair work. I'd always be near to help you." He took a deep breath and unloaded his biggest problem. "You've got to go, Niki, because I can't go alone. I'm nearly broke."

"So am I," Niki confessed. He explained the financial arrangement Mr. Barnard had set up, and how his two dollars spending money seemed to melt away week by week.

"Two dollars a week!" Jokey exploded. "You mean he only pays you two dollars a week? Gosh, if you're not crazy to stay another day with anybody like that. How do you know he'll come across with the rest of it? He's got no right to make you work unless he pays you. It's against the law."

"I can trust Mr. Barnard. He'll pay me all I'm worth." Niki remembered the small gray pelt that had lain enfolded in layers of tissue paper. He was the one who should pay. Actually Mr. Barnard owed him nothing.

Jokey interrupted his thoughts, explaining that they wouldn't need much money anyway. He had a rope and a set of tools in the trunk, and whenever they saw a car in trouble, they would stop and help. They could change tires for people, or give them a tow.

"Then they'll give us a tip," he concluded, "and we can pick up hitchhikers and they'll pay for the gas, and as soon as you're used to driving, you can drive while I sleep, and I'll drive while you sleep. We'll be there in two or three days."

It sounded easy, this way of traveling west to see the United States. And with Jokey's father and a job at the end of the journey it certainly was the chance of a lifetime.

Niki shook his head. "I'm sorry, Jokey, but I can't do it. I got into trouble once this summer and Mr. Barnard gave me one more chance to make good. I've got to stick it out here."

"Okay for you," Jokey said, looking at him scornfully. "You've changed all right. You didn't used to be afraid to take a chance on anything. But me, I'm getting away. I'm not going back to Warren." Jokey's face was grim. "I'll get along somehow, and I'm starting tonight." He looked out the window and sighed. "It looks like a long way though, all alone."

Niki felt uncomfortable. What ought he to do? He couldn't let an old pal down. Jokey was his best friend. And he should be with his father. His grandmother and grandfather were so old they didn't want a fellow to have any fun. Jokey'd had it pretty tough, living with them.

"I'm not saying I've changed my mind," he began, "but if I should decide to go there are some things I want to know. I don't want to get into any more trouble."

The speed with which Jokey produced a wallet full of papers, and turned towards Niki with hope shining like a beacon in his eyes, made Niki squirm.

"You mean my license," Jokey said. "There it is. The inspector at the Registry of Motor Vehicles gave me the works and I passed. He said I was good."

"Joseph Perry," Niki read, casting an inquiring glance upward. "But your name is Joaquim. And your birthday is October, not July."

"So what?" Jokey asked. "It came early this year, that's all."

It was a poor attempt at a joke, and it fell flat under Niki's searching eyes.

"Listen, if I tell you everything, will you go with me?" Jokey pleaded. "Honest, Niki, I don't want to go alone. But you and me together, we'd get along all right."

Niki was touched. There was no doubt Jokey needed him.

"Is the car insured and everything?"

It was. Niki looked at the papers. Insured and registered to Arthur Perry, the fellow at the garage. Jokey explained that Arthur wanted to help him get to his father. He had loaned Jokey the birth certificate of his younger brother, because, he said, there were dozens of Joe Perrys with fathers named Manuel, and Arthur knew Jokey was a good driver, ready for a license. So the car had been registered and insured by him, with Jokey paying the bills.

"I paid him fifty dollars for doing it," Jokey owned up, "and I signed a paper that if I have an accident that costs him money, I promise to pay it back. But we aren't going to have accidents. I've got no use for crazy drivers. I drive careful and I obey the laws."

It sounded all right. He and Jokey looked to be
sixteen. What difference did a few months make,
anyway? They could reach Denver all right. He
could write notes to his mother and the Barnards explaining Jokey's need of him, and he could even
promise to return by train when he earned money for
his fare. There was nothing really wrong about
going.

Trying to read his thoughts, Jokey watched the
wrinkles deepen in Niki's forehead. "Nobody's going
to hold it against us as long as they know we're on the
level. Garage mechanics get two dollars and up an
hour. You'll soon be sending money home, and before long you'll have a car of your own."

Like a pendulum, Niki's thoughts swung back
and forth, from the Barnards to the uranium mines
in Colorado; from his mother to Jokey's dad. He
tried to see the whole picture, present and future, before making his decision.

"How did you get away from the place where you
work?" he asked.

"Mr. Donelly, he's the one I live with and he
owns the garage, he gave me three days off. He's all
right. I like him. He gave me a lot of parts for my
car, and he lets me use his tools whenever I want to."
His eyes met Niki's and slid off again. "He doesn't

know about the license. He thinks I'm at Arthur's summer cottage."

"What's he going to say when Arthur goes back without you?"

Jokey shrugged his shoulders and slid down onto the middle of his spine. "I don't know. I'll be half-way to Denver by that time. I'm going to write to my father that I'm on the way. You're coming, aren't you, Niki? We won't break laws. We'll be careful all the time."

Niki sucked the last sweet drops from the coke bottle.

"Let me think it over until tonight. You park on the woods road near the pond. Try to get some sleep. I'll see you around midnight, as soon as the Barnards go to bed." A pulse like a hammer pounded in his head; an uncomfortable tightness writhed in his stomach; another to match it hurt in his chest. It was the same old fight against indecision, the torn-two-ways feeling that always tormented him when he had to make up his mind.

They drove back to the pond and Jokey let him out.

"I'll be right here waiting for you. I'm going back to the Post Office now and write to Dad. You and me together, old pal!" Jokey sang out as he spun the car around on the narrow road.

"Listen, Jokey, I didn't promise anything," Niki called after him, too late, for Jokey had disappeared, and only a cloud of dry, choking dust showed where his car had been.

Chapter 13   WATERS UNDER THE EARTH

Niki ran up the driveway, past the chinchillas' house and the garden and across the lawn to stand for a moment under a great elm and look at the view he loved. He had to get hold of himself before he could talk to anybody. Nothing seemed real any more, not even Hercules who nearly tipped him over, demanding attention.

Was it possible that tomorrow at this time he might be hundreds of miles away?

He knelt to rub the dog behind his ears, and to scratch the place that was hard for Herky to reach

in front of his stubby tail. The boxer writhed in ec-
stasy and begged for more as Niki started back towards the house. The rattle of dishes told him supper
was under way. Hot biscuits, probably. He sighed,
for if he went away with Jokey he would certainly
miss Mrs. Barnard's cooking. Feeling the need of
doing something, he filled an old tin can half full of
kerosene and started for the grapevines to drown a
few hundred Japanese beetles. He worked mechani-
cally, tapping the leaves, and catching the cursed
insects as they fell until Mrs. Barnard called him to
come and wash up. Supper was ready.

During the meal, conversation centered on Sam
Bumpus, for he had promised to come tonight to find
water for the new well. Niki tried to keep his mind on
what they were saying about Sam's exploits, and
about men who could find water by using their rod
over the map of a place a thousand miles away. Niki
didn't believe it, but it might be true, for wasn't he
leaving for Denver in a few hours! If anybody had
told him that last night, he would have thought it
impossible.

After supper he did the chores quickly and went
to the pond. The thought that this might be his last
swim started his stomach churning again. There was
no sign of Jokey or his car, so Niki flung himself
into the water. He was going to miss this. He wished

he could wait a day, two days, to think it over before deciding. But there could be no waiting. Tonight, or never. He wanted to go terribly, and at the same time he didn't want to. He swam hard and fast. The tension did not lessen.

After a quick swim, Niki came home to find Sam's car in the yard, and at the corner of the pasture he saw him with Mr. Barnard. Sam had a forked stick in his hands, the two long ends held firmly, the short end of the Y pointing straight ahead.

"Are you doing it?" Niki shouted, racing across the yard. "Have you found the water already?"

Sam Bumpus shook his head, his eyes twinkling under the shaggy brows.

"Is there any water on this farm?" he asked, speaking to the stick.

The point of the rod dipped.

"How many veins? One?" It dipped again. "Two?" The rod said yes. "Three?" It didn't move.

"You've got water. Two veins. Good strong pull. Now we'll find out where."

Sam faced north and boxed the compass, turning with the stick as he named each direction. "North, north by east, north northeast; northeast by north, northeast by east; east northeast, east by north, east." Solemn as an owl he continued naming, and turning. The rod dipped slightly at northeast; at south by east it turned down so hard it squeaked in his hands.

Niki grinned. "You're giving me a good time, aren't you!"

"Mebbe," Sam replied, looking at him thoughtfully. "Mebbe I am and mebbe I ain't." He turned to Mr. Barnard. "You've got a pretty fair vein to the northeast, but your big one is to the south'ard."

"It's the first vein that feeds the present well. I know where those springs are."

The men turned to the southeast and Niki trailed after them. Across the meadows and over stone walls they went, Sam keeping his arms close to his sides, and holding the rod in front of him. Suddenly he stopped.

"Got it," he said. Back and forth, over rocks and through knee-deep grass and underbrush he tramped. "Drop a rock there, boy," he told Niki, kicking away the grass. Niki grabbed a stone from the wall and dropped it on the spot. Sam continued to walk back and forth in all directions. His stick pointed downward whenever he came near the place Niki had marked.

"This is it all right," he said. "One vein runs deep down this side to the pond, and the smaller one seems to cross it here. You'll get all the water you need, around fifteen gallons a minute, I'd say, about ten feet down." Once again he walked in a widening circle, and returned to walk across the stone. "Yup. It's a good strong pull."

"Can I try it and see if the stick will move for me?" Niki asked.

"Sure. Cut yourself a stick."

"What kind?"

"Any kind. Maple's good, or cherry, birch, apple. Witch hazel when you can find it." He passed his knife to Niki, who cut a Y shaped branch from a small maple. Holding it in his upturned hands, arms close to his sides, Niki walked across the area marked by the stone just as Sam had done. Nothing happened. Disappointed, he tried again and again as the men talked about scoop shovels and clam shells.

"Have you tried it, Mr. Barnard?" Niki asked.

"It doesn't work for me. Only one in five hundred can feel the pull."

"I felt it a little," Niki said, "but the stick didn't turn."

"Here, take hold of one end," Sam Bumpus said, extending his rod towards Niki, and grasping the boy's right hand in his own left. "Do it with me, and tell me when you feel anything." They walked a short distance away from the stone and then across a pdace of trampled grass.

"It's here. I do feel it!" Niki shouted as the rod twisted in his fingers. "Jeepers! Let's do it again.

Let's go back over the place where we put the stone."

"Go ahead," Sam said. "I'm tired and I'm going home." He turned to Mr. Barnard. "If we can get Taber's scoop shovel I'll come back with him tomorrow morning. It won't take long. And if we don't find water, it's up to me as usual."

Seeing the curious look on Niki's face, Mr. Barnard explained that Sam always offered to pay the cost of operation if no water was found where he said it would be. His promise might involve hundreds of dollars for the drilling when the vein was deep.

"When Sam says water's there, it's there. And they've got to reach it if they drill straight. So far as I know, he's never lost a penny."

Long after Sam had gone, Mr. Barnard and Niki talked about it, this uncanny, mysterious thing called water dowsing. But so was radio mysterious, and television, and finding microbes, and splitting atoms.

"It's a wonderful age we're living in," Mr. Barnard said with the kind of easy friendliness that removed the barrier between them.

"I know it," Niki answered. He stayed in the kitchen while Mr. Barnard started preparations for feeding the chinchillas. "Can I go with you tonight?"

"You'd better go to bed. You'll have quite a day tomorrow, I expect."

It was like a prophecy. Niki looked up, startled,

but Mr. Barnard was stacking plates, his face expressionless.

"Good night," Niki said.

"Good night."

When he reached his room, he closed the door and sat down on the bed to think. He had to make the decision. Now. If he didn't go this time he might never get another chance. Jokey looked to him for help. Jokey, his old pal. He'd had a tough time of it. He needed his father.

The wrong part would be leaving without telling the Barnards. But they would stop him and Jokey, too. It wasn't running away. Neither of them had done anything wrong to run away from. Niki counted his money. $3.56. It was all he had. He began to pack his bag, still telling himself it was not too late to get out of going, for he hadn't promised Jokey anything.

Mr. Barnard came in, came upstairs, and closed the door to his room. Niki listened intently. At last the house was still. It was time to go. With his bag held high so that it wouldn't bump the stairs, he made his way to the porch. He decided to wait there an hour so that if they had heard him it would arouse no suspicions. And the outside screen door had a latch that clicked. Wait an hour. That was the way to play it safe.

As he sat on the porch sofa, with Hercules at his

knee, the excitement waned and drowsiness flooded
in. It had been a long, busy day, and his healthy
body demanded its usual rest. He dared not lie down,
but he leaned his head against the pillows and closed
his eyes. The clock struck twelve. It was already tomorrow, but for five minutes he must rest.

The startled call of a bird in the darkness awak-
ened him. What had frightened it, he wondered, a
prowling cat, a squirrel? Had it opened its eyes to
find death staring at it in its nest? He shivered. Did
it mean something, waking like that? He looked at
his watch. Two A.M. He must go. Now.

For a while he sat there, holding his head in his
hands, his elbows on his knees. Why was making this
decision so hard for him? Was it because all his life
he had done the easy thing, without thinking about
the right or wrong of it, or the consequences? The
weak link, Mr. Barnard had called it. But he couldn't
let Jokey down. What kind of friend would he be
to let a pal start off alone on a journey like that. Jokey
had come to him for help. He couldn't face him and
say, "Sorry, but I've changed my mind." As soon
as they got going the excitement of the adventure
would wipe out all these doubts that bothered him.
He was sure of that.

As he closed the door as quietly as he could, he
thought of all he was leaving behind. Of June. The old

unanswered questions came to mind: Why had she
told Toby? How had her father found out so much
about the gang in Warren? Why had she changed so?
She was so — so like the moonlight, the starlight —
he remembered his words, that night as she sat in the
boat facing him, so near, the water sparkling as it
dripped from her fingers. Well, it was over. He'd
send her a postcard from Denver. She'd be surprised.

He thought of the chinchillas and the ranch he
was going to have, of his twins. He hadn't seen them
for over two weeks. He thought of Hooper. Well,
he could make good in Denver as well as any place if
he was willing to work, and he was. When he and
Jokey discovered a uranium deposit it would mean
plenty of money . . .

He walked across the grass. It was very quiet, as
though the whole world in silence was watching him
go. He stopped a minute to look up at the stars, so
many millions of them, each traveling according to
a plan.

Tears backed up in his nose as he stared." What's
it all about? What is right and what is wrong? What
am I going to do?" It was a queer prayer, if it was
a prayer, but no questions could have been a more
sincere cry for help.

The answer came. You promised your mother
you'd make good. You promised Mr. Morgan you'd

stick it out all summer. You promised Mr. Barnard
. . . you promised yourself. And promises are to keep.
Talk to Jokey. Make him wait a year, and save up
money, and when you both have licenses and everything about the registration is legal, and you are
under no obligations to Mr. Morgan or anybody, then
you can go. His thoughts raced on as he hid his bag in
the shrubbery and walked toward the car.

Jokey was waiting impatiently.

"Gosh, I thought you'd never come. I was afraid
you'd let me down." It was a lonely spot he had chos-
en for his vigil, and the night sounds, the rustlings
and squeakings, the shadows moving, the dampness
from the pond, the mosquitoes, had all combined to
keep him wide awake and jittery. "Where's your
bag?"

"It's back at the Barnards. Listen. I've got to
talk to you. There are some reasons why I can't go."

"Okay. So you're yellow. You're scared. Afraid
to take a chance. That's the kind of a pal you are. I
might have known it and not wasted twelve hours
looking you up."

"Listen to me, Jokey, and then say it. Your license isn't valid. Neither of us is old enough to drive.
The registration and insurance are made out to another guy. Let some cop ask to see the license and ask
a few questions and we're sunk. And you'll need

money. You can't be sure you'll get tips. I've only got
a little over three dollars. We might go without eating but you've got to buy gas and oil, and you
couldn't get far on three dollars."

Cool mist from the pond fogged the windows of
the car. Jokey took a cloth and began to clean them.

"I'm going," he said. " I made up my mind and
I'm going."

"Wait till next year and I'll go with you. We'll
be sixteen and we'll have money and travel right. If
you start without money people are going to ask you
questions. Suppose you come to a toll road and you
haven't got the price? Suppose you run out of gas or
blow a tire? You can stick it out a little longer, Jokey.
What's Mr. Morgan going to say if you go off like this
after he found that good place for you to keep you out
of reform school?"

"Listen, why don't you go be a priest or a min-
ister or something? I said I was going to Denver,
didn't I? I'm not going back to Warren. I'm going to
Denver. I'm starting now." He stepped on the starter.

Niki took the bills from his wallet and fished out
a handful of loose change from his pocket.

"Take it, Jokey," he said. "It's all I have. It will
help a little. Let me know how you make out."

"I don't want your money," Jokey answered, but
he took it.

Feeling like a traitor, Niki turned away. The soft purring of the motor changed to a vibrant hum as Jokey eased into high and was off. Niki watched the car disappear in the distance. Now, when it was too late, he wished he had gone. He felt flat, lonely, defeated. The stars still shone brightly as he walked across the road to the Barnards', but Niki didn't see them. He picked up his bag with a sigh, let himself in quietly, went to his room, got into bed. He felt as though he had been through a wringer, but in two minutes he was asleep.

Dimly, from a distance, he heard a voice calling his name, and after several blinking attempts, he opened his eyes. It was broad daylight and Mrs. Barnard was standing beside his bed, shaking him gently.

"Niki, are you all right? You slept right through your alarm. And now it's eight o'clock, and I called you several times."

He fought his way back to consciousness and rubbed his eyes.

"I'm all right. I guess I overslept." He yawned and tried to remember what had happened. His head ached. In fact he ached all over. There was an all-gone feeling inside him. His eyes focussed on the open suitcase on the chair beside the bed, just as he had left it when he pulled out his pajamas at three o'clock that morning. If Mrs. Barnard noticed it, she said nothing and kept her own counsel.

After breakfast Niki felt better. By the time the scoop shovel arrived, he was on his toes with excitement. He helped Sam and Mr. Barnard tear down part of the stone wall and pile flat stones so that they could be used for shoring up the hole where the pool would be.

The big unwieldy machine lumbered across the meadows, stopping near the spot marked by Niki's stone. Mr. Taber swung it into place and it bit into the dry, gravelly soil. A more unlikely place for hidden streams to be running was never seen. The digging continued until they had made a storage basin about eighty feet long and thirty feet wide. Once Sam jumped into the hole with his rod, to test again, and confirmed his statement that water was near. For twenty minutes more the digging continued, and then a stream of water as big as a man's arm burst out of the side of the pit.

"Just hook a pump on that," Sam said, "and you've got your irrigating system."

Niki watched as the water poured into the hole. "What's going to stop it?" he asked. "Won't it overflow? Then you'll lose it all."

"It will overflow, except when you have the pumps going. But it won't be wasted, because it seeps back into the ground. It looks as though you and I will have some digging to do."

Niki was speechless. The rod, back there by the pasture fence, had told the truth.

"Going to pace it off and get your order in for a steel pipe?" Sam asked. "They're slower than cold molasses sending stuff when you need it quick."

"You're right," Charles Barnard agreed, "but I'm one up on you this time, Sam. I sent in the order in the morning mail."

The men and the scoop shovel started back toward the house, while Niki found the dowsing rod he had cut the night before, and with it in his hands, tramped back and forth across the field for another half hour, trying in vain to feel a pull towards hidden running waters.

Chapter 14 **STORMY WEATHER**

The answer to some of the questions that had disturbed Niki for so long came the following afternoon when, on reaching Indian Pond, he found Patty waiting for him. She looked excited as she pulled a letter from her beach bag.

"It's for you, Niki, from June," she said, handing it to him. "You know she's been at the camp all summer, but I saw her last Saturday. She thought you had gone away and she felt terrible about it."

Niki looked at the envelope. The flap was stuck down and sealed with three stickers.

"It's terribly private," Patty explained.

Niki had an intuitive flash that probably she had read it. Maybe she had helped June write it. You could never tell about girls!

Patty went on, "Some people think June is shallow, you know, frivolous, and well, kind of crazy acting, but she isn't really. She's very deep and oh, Niki, she thinks you're terrific." She looked at him with such earnestness and admiration that Niki grinned in spite of himself. He'd said it! You could never tell about girls.

"Yuh? Well, thanks."

"Aren't you going to read it?"

"Sure I'm going to read it. By and by."

His first and only letter from June. He had to be alone when he read it. He strolled over to the lower end of the cove. June liked him. He wasn't so sure of his present feelings for her. He would have liked to blame her for all his troubles, but he couldn't, honestly. If he hadn't boasted so much, and well, lied a little, she would never have insisted on his opening the chinchilla cage. Probably the letter explained why she had told Toby. He frowned at the envelope, then ripped through the seals.

"Dear Niki," it began, "I know you can never forgive me for telling my father, but I had to. It was Toby we heard in the bushes that night and after he heard us talking he kept threatening to tell my father about your showing me the chinchillas unless I would go dancing with him. And my father never would let me go on dates alone with him, so I had to say I was going somewhere else. It was awful. You can't imagine how awful to keep lying and lying about it. And when my father did find out he started to bawl Toby out, and Toby told him everything he had heard you say that night. Then my father was so mad he called your Mr. Morgan and the Warren police station. But I believe in you, Niki, and I always will. Next week I'm going to Patty's. Meet me at the pond at three o'clock on Thursday. Please, I've got to see you. June."

Niki read it twice before he got the whole meaning. Toby! It was Toby they had heard crashing through the underbrush when Mr. Simmons came down to the boat. And June hadn't told Toby anything. A weight like a ton of bricks lifted from Niki's heart. But gosh! He'd like to get his hands on Toby. He clenched his fist and flexed the muscles of his lean brown arm. His eyes glinted as he brought a swift jab with his right and followed with a deadly left hook to an imaginary jaw. He'd give him what he deserved, the big sneak.

But first he had to find him. It was weeks since

Toby had been to Indian Pond. Maybe June knew where he was. The thought of his forcing her to go on dates with him made Niki see red.

"I'll find him and beat him up if it's the last thing I ever do," he muttered. He saw Patty coming his way, and being in no mood to share his thoughts with her, folded the letter tightly in his hand and rushed into the water. On the far side of the pond he buried the soggy pieces in the sand.

Hot, sultry days followed one another. Still the weather forecasts gave no promise of rain. In places where there was no shade, the lawn had already burned brown and dry as a camel's back. The small water holes in the pasture had long since dried up.

Sam Bumpus' reservoir was full, overflowing in a clear cold stream about two feet wide and a couple of inches deep. Shallow trenches were dug across the pasture to the vegetable and flower gardens to send water where it was needed, but the pipes to carry it had not arrived. In the meantime, Niki and Mr. Barnard trundled cans of water in a wheelbarrow to fill tubs for the cows, and carried more cans to the barn and the gardens where flowers and vegetables wilted under the scorching sun. Gasping for breath, Lydia and the other hens huddled in the shade. All the farmers in Bristol watched the sky in vain for clouds that might bring showers to save their crops.

"Come on, rain," Niki said. "Any day but Thursday."

But no rain came. Thursday, like the other days, dawned hot and humid. By ten o'clock the thermometer registered ninety in the shade. The air was heavy and oppressive, smelling faintly of woodsmoke from distant forest fires. Every movement made Niki drip with sweat.

Mr. Barnard was no longer using his dwindling water supply to wet down the roof of the chinchilla house. Instead he carried in huge cakes of ice, his face crimson with exertion.

"Can't I do that for you?" Niki asked.

"You keep out of the chinchilla house. I'll do it," Mr. Barnard answered. He was worried, desperately worried, Niki knew; impatient and angry with the pipe company; in no mood for talking. So Niki said no more.

Early in the afternoon white clouds began to pile up in the northwest. Distant thunder rolled continuously. In the south there was blue sky; in the northwest it was dull, ominous gray. Ragged wisps of cloud broke away and scudded before the rising wind. A sudden loud reverberation seemed to climb the sky and explode directly over Bristol, then go growling down the sky again. And still no rain.

For an hour they watched and waited. At last, Mr. Barnard, wise in the ways of weather, said to Niki, "This is it. Get the cows while I shut up the buildings."

In a few minutes it grew dark. The wind changed, blowing in furious gusts. Niki ran down the lane and found the cows waiting at the bars. Thunder rolled louder; flashes of lightning flickered through the dark clouds like opening and closing shutters, Niki thought. And even then it didn't rain.

He wondered whether June would keep her date. He thought she would. She usually did what she wanted to. As he entered the kitchen, Mrs. Barnard called, "Take in the clothes, Niki. They aren't dry, but the wind will whip them to pieces even if it doesn't rain."

"Okay. In a minute." He looked at the clock. Five minutes of three. The clouds were lifting a little. A queer half-light replaced the lowering darkness. He'd run down to the pond first and see if June was there. It wasn't going to rain quite yet. The clothes could wait a few minutes.

He found the beach deserted, the water lead-colored. Leaves whipped off the trees in the sudden gusts of wind. Well, he hadn't exactly expected June, but he was disappointed. In fact, his feet were like weights that were hard to move as he walked back to the road to watch another minute. Then he saw her in the distance, tearing along on her bicycle. His heart thumped fast and hard as he stood there waiting.

"Oh, Niki, I can't stay," she said in greeting, "I'm supposed to be at the store. They say it's going to be an awful storm and I have to get back. I hate thunder storms." She shivered and looked at the angry sky.

Niki was speechless. He couldn't take his eyes from her as she stood there, her golden hair blowing in the wind.

"You're not mad at me? she asked. "Tell me you're not mad."

"No. Of course not."

"When do you go back?"

"The day after Labor Day. June, have you seen Toby again?" He saw the color deepen in her face.

"No, and I never want to."

"I'm going to see him again." Something in Niki's voice and the grim expression on his face frightened June.

"No, Niki, don't. Please don't."

"Where is he?"

"I don't know."

"Yes, you do."

"Honest, Niki. He lost his job on the golf course.

He is driving a truck and working at an inn somewhere, but I don't know where. You mustn't go looking for him. It will only get you into more trouble."

Rumbling thunder gave notice that the storm was
coming nearer.

"I'm going to see him," Niki repeated. "I'm going
to make him get down on his knees and promise he'll
never look at you again." The more he talked about it,
the braver he felt. Sure, Toby was bigger, but at
the Athletic Club in Warren Niki had boxed older,
bigger boys. And with June to fight for — well, he'd
show her!

She read his thoughts as she watched his face.

"You're wonderful, Niki, but I don't want you to
fight over me. Please don't." Her eyes were pleading.
"It's all over now. He won't bother me again."

"He's a rat, a sneaking — "

"I know that. But it won't change him to have
you go around looking for him and fighting him."
She dropped her eyes, a little smile playing around
her lips. "He knows he hasn't got a chance with me.
Nobody has but you, Niki."

Niki's heart knocked against his ribs with a heavy
thud, thud, thud, while all the things he wanted to say
to her went flying away with the wind. The long,
low rumble of the thunder, like the final salute in a

distant fireworks display, might have been the buzzing of a mosquito for all he cared. But June heard it
and shivered.

"Oh, Niki, I've got to go. Write to me. I'll never
forget you. Never." She wheeled her bicycle around
as she talked. "Well, goodbye."

"So long," he said. And she was gone. Never in
all his life had Niki felt so alone. He stood in the
road and watched her disappear in the distance. He
hadn't remembered one of the nice things he'd wanted
to say. He wished he'd kissed her. June wasn't silly
like other girls. She was, well, she was different.

He saw with astonishment that his arms, his
clothes, the road, everything was wet. The rain was
coming down in earnest, the drops as big as quarters.
He walked slowly back to the house.

The wash was still on the line. But before Niki
reached it he saw Mr. and Mrs. Barnard. She was in
a heap on the steps. He was bending over her.

"Where in Heaven's name have you been?" Mr.
Barnard asked.

"What happened? Is she hurt?"

"She fell. Head first down the steps. Dizzy with
the heat I suppose. And of course you'd never be
around when you're needed to help."

Niki knew. She was going to take in the clothes.

His face contracted with the pain of it. He had failed again.

Mrs. Barnard touched his hand.

"My flowers, Niki. My dahlias and tall mari-golds. I wanted to pick them, before the wind." She said it softly. To comfort him . . . even though she was in pain.

"I'm awfully sorry."

He helped Mr. Barnard carry her to the bed hammock on the porch.

"How do you feel now?" her husband asked.

"I'm all right. Except my ankle. I twisted it."

Niki fanned her and gave her a drink of water while Mr. Barnard telephoned for the doctor. Her breath came in uneasy gasps; a vein like a little blue hill jumped in her wrist. The twisted ankle had swollen to twice its normal size.

"Cold compresses will help that," Niki said. "As soon as Mr. Barnard gets through talking to the doctor, I'll help him put them on. We'll wring out cloths in ice water and it will feel good to you."

She smiled at him. "All right, Niki."

"You know I'm sorry . . . about the wash." Niki's voice did funny things sometimes, growling, and squeaking. It did it now, and it was hard to keep it steady.

"Don't worry. I know you meant to do it."

Mr. Barnard returned to the room. "Do you feel able to go to the doctor's? He wants to take X-rays."

With Niki's help, he got her into the car, her face drawn with pain, but still insisting she was all right. Niki fervently hoped she was. She looked so little and so frail.

A heavy clap of thunder shook the ground. Lightning flashed from every direction.

"It's going to be a humdinger, Niki. Look out for everything. We'll get back as soon as we can."

Mr. Barnard released the brakes and the car rolled down the driveway. For the second time that day Niki felt terribly alone.

Chapter 15 **BROKEN PROMISE**

Niki took in the clothes and spread them on the drying rods in the kitchen. He picked the tall marigolds and zinnias and put them in vases before the storm broke in all its fury, with howling wind and torrents of rain. Lightning crackled, followed by earth-shaking thunder. It was as dark as night.

Unable to sit still, Niki walked from room to room wondering what he should do if the next bolt hit the house. Or the barn. It was stiflingly hot with the windows closed, yet his teeth were chattering and his hands clammy cold.

All the afternoon it rained with intermittent thunder. The air did not clear. Instead it grew hotter and stickier. At supper time Niki fed the animals and forced himself to eat some cereal. He swallowed a few mouthfuls and gave the rest to Hercules.

Why didn't the Barnards come home? Why didn't they telephone? Was it because Mrs. Barnard was hurt — not just her ankle, but internally, like Hooper?

He couldn't stand not knowing. He tried to call the doctor's office. When he removed the receiver there was no dial tone. That meant the lines were down . . . no way of getting help if lightning should strike. Feeling lonelier than before, he did the barn chores, milked Brownie and Bess, strained the milk and put the cans in the cooler. He washed the milk pails, scalded the cloths. It helped to be working. He wished he could get to the chinchillas. Were they disturbed by the roar of thunder, he wondered. Had the ice cakes melted? Oh, if only the Barnards would come home.

In the early evening came a second storm, this time without warning. There was a crack like a pistol shot followed by a crash of thunder that rocked the house. All the lights went out. Niki groped his way upstairs to find his flashlight. There was another flash so close his fingers tingled with the shock, and

another, and another. He was sure the house had
been struck. With knees trembling he crept up the
steep stairs to the tiny attic. He cringed as a cobweb
brushed his face. It was unbearably hot up there but
everything looked all right.

Maybe it was the barn! He went outdoors, fighting against the wind as it tore great branches from
the Norway maple trees. He rolled the barn door
open and slipped through, climbed to the haymow
and sniffed for smoke. There was nothing wrong.

Pulling on Mr. Barnard's old rubber coat, he
walked around the chinchilla house. With the power
gone, the electric fans would stop. Thirty thousand
dollars worth of chinchillas could faint and die if they
got too hot. He rubbed his wet hands together nervously. If only the key were where it used to be, how
easy to go in and make sure that everything was all
right.

Niki had never known hours to pass so slowly.
Nine o'clock, ten o'clock, eleven, twelve, slowly the
hours tolled, and still the Barnards did not return.
The rain stopped and Niki opened doors and windows
to the cool air. He tried to read by candlelight. It
was no use. He lay down on the divan and tried to
sleep. He could not lie still. He got up again and
paced back and forth, back and forth.

He couldn't help thinking about the chinchillas.

It was hours past feeding time . . . and so hot. Every window had been closed while the fans were blowing the ice-cooled air. But all the ice would have melted hours ago. The rain had probably helped to cool the place a little. Niki wished he could be sure. He would have given anything in the world to be able to help Mr. Morgan and Nikita, Chica, and Ande and their little baby.

He stared into the darkness. Zigzag chains of lightning still tore at the black sky. Low rumblings of thunder reverberated, farther and farther away. Rain dripped from every leaf and ran down the gutter spouts. The heavy sweetness of Mrs. Barnard's petunias and nicotianas mingled with the smell of the wet earth.

Niki pulled out a chair and sat down. Hearing the sound, Hercules came to lean his wet body against the boy's legs. He knew something was wrong — not just the noise that hurt his sensitive ears, but something else besides. He put his head on Niki's knee and asked as plainly as though he used words, "Where are my master and mistress?"

"I don't know where they are, Herky," Niki answered. "I can't understand why they haven't come. They should have been back hours ago. Unless it's Mrs. Barnard." The fear hurt in his throat again as he rubbed the dog's head. "Oh, Herky, don't let it be that."

To prove no harm would ever befall Mrs. Barnard if Niki had anything to do with it, the boxer put his paws on the boy's shoulders and tried to lick his face. Niki's head ached with weariness as he leaned against the dog's wet coat.

"We've got to do something about the chinchillas. If only I could know what is right and what is wrong."

He took hold of Hercules' legs and made him get down. Together they walked to the chinchilla house. Wouldn't Mr. Barnard want him to go in this time? He could quiet the little animals if they were frightened. He could open windows and let in the cool, refreshing air. Wasn't it right this time to break his promise?

Again he walked around the building. The small-paned windows were screened and locked. One door was bolted from the inside; the other had a Yale lock. Could he get in by the chimney? No good. There was only one way: to smash the door panel near the lock, reach in and lift the button.

Then what, if the animals were all right? If he smashed the door and it was not necessary, wouldn't Mr. Barnard sound off! Niki wanted these last weeks

to go smoothly. He wanted the Barnards to have
something good to tell his mother if she came. It
would be terrible to get sent home tomorrow. And it
could happen.

"Herky, it's like this," he said, after examining
the door panels, "I promised not to go in. Promises
are to keep. He said that himself. Had I better leave
it? If the chinchillas die from the heat I can say,
'So what? It wasn't up to me to do anything. You
told me to keep out and I did.'"

Herky lifted his head and listened, trying to
understand.

"He's needled me plenty of times." No, that
wasn't fair. "It was my fault every time. He was good
to let me stay . . . after Hooper. If I went in and
saved the herd, wouldn't that make up for it? Herky,
I'm going to do it. If it isn't the right way, I'll take
the consequences."

It was good to wait a minute, holding the dog in
his arms. Then he went to the woodshed, got the
hatchet and swung it twice against the panel of the
door close to the lock. Reaching through the splint-
ered hole, he released the catch.

"Stay there, boy," he said to Hercules as he
stepped inside, hooking the screen door. Compared
with the outside air it was hot and stuffy in the building. The animals were quiet, evidently unharmed.

Niki flashed his light on the thermometer. 82°. Nothing dangerous about that. A cold chill ran down his spine. Had he made a mistake? If he had, he might as well start packing.

He tried to center his thoughts on what he was doing as he opened windows and measured pellets. It would do no good to think about what Mr. Barnard was going to say when he saw the broken door.

As he opened the first cage to place a paper saucer of pellets inside, he noticed his flashlight was growing dim. There would be no time for feeding, he decided. In the minute of light that was left, he looked for his twins, but before he could find them, the wires glowed dimly and went out.

He felt his way back to the door and stepped outside to look at the stars that pricked through the darkness, but they brought no joy to him. Never in his life had he felt so worried, so tired, so completely discouraged.

"Stay there, Herky," he told the dog, as he hooked the screen door. Then, because there was no chair in the chinchilla house, and because he could not leave it unlocked, he sat down on some empty grain bags and leaned his head against the wall. He heard the grandfather clock strike one before he fell asleep.

He awoke to the sound of voices and a bright light

shining in his eyes. Mr. Barnard was banging on the screen door and calling, "Niki, Niki, are you all right? Let me in."

Niki moved his stiff legs and scrambled to his feet. "How is Mrs. Barnard?" he asked as he opened the door.

In the glow of the headlights he could see a woman coming toward him, but she was too large to be Mrs. Barnard. It looked like, but it couldn't possibly be — yes, it was. His mother!

"Mom!" he cried in astonishment, giving her a bear hug that almost cracked her ribs. "How did you get here?" He looked from her to Mr. Barnard, unbelieving.

"And how did *you* get here?" Mr. Barnard asked. "What in the world were you doing, sleeping in the chinchilla house?"

"I'll tell you everything in a minute," Niki answered, "but where is Mrs. Barnard? Didn't she come home?"

"It was a bad sprain and she'll have to stay in the hospital a couple of days," Mr. Barnard explained. "Even when she comes home she'll have to be careful. So, as long as we'd asked your mother to come, I telephoned her to come right away. Luckily the line to Warren was still working. And she's going to keep house for us until Martha gets over the worst of it."

"But how did you get here?" Niki asked his mother.

"I flew."

He rubbed his eyes. He still couldn't believe it.

"How's Granny?"

"She's fine. She was as excited as I was when Mr. Barnard telephoned. Then I called my boss to see if I could leave right away."

"Mr. Lemos?" Niki asked, remembering. "I bet he said yes."

His mother nodded, smiling. "He did, so I packed my bag in a hurry and took a taxi to the airport. But most of the planes were grounded on account of the storm. I couldn't get word to Mr. Barnard because he'd gone back to the hospital when he found everything was off schedule. So I waited in Warren, and he waited in Bristol until my plane did get in at eleven thirty. Then he met me."

Mr. Barnard picked up the story, telling how he had to make six detours to get home from the airport. A dam had given way, a bridge was washed out, and the streets along the river were under water. Trees were down, blocking roads everywhere.

"How was it here?" he asked. "I've never seen anything like it except in a hurricane. In fact, it was a hurricane in some places. Did you get along all right? I tried to telephone, but all the local lines are down for miles around."

Niki told them of his long night's vigil, of his concern for the chinchillas and his decision to see that they were all right. He kept his eyes on Mr. Barnard's face as he talked. Maybe he had used poor judgment, but he was not ashamed of what he had done. That was something.

He turned to his mother. "I haven't told you this, but for certain reasons I promised not to go into the chinchilla house. But chinchillas faint and sometimes die from the heat. I knew the ice had melted and that the fans would stop when we lost power."

"What time was that?" Mr. Barnard asked.

"Half past seven. So I thought if they were dying in there for lack of fresh air, I could save them and that I ought to do it. So I got an axe and smashed the door."

"Oh, Niki!" said his mother looking anxiously from one face to the other. "You shouldn't have done that."

"If I did wrong I'm sorry. But it wasn't the weak link breaking this time." His face was pale with weariness, but he met Mr. Barnard's eyes squarely and unflinchingly.

"It probably was not necessary," Mr. Barnard

said, examining the door. "But I believe you, Niki.
You thought it was. And it took courage to break
your promise. How did you find them? Everything all
right?"

"Yes. I opened the windows. I would have fed
them, but my flashlight went dead."

Mr. Barnard gave him the slow, kind smile, like
the old days.

"We'll mend the door panel first thing in the
morning. Or the second thing. I suppose the first
thing you will want to do is to show your mother
Nikita and Mr. Morgan."

Niki's face brightened. "You bet," he said.

Mrs. Louganis smiled at him. She did not understand the significance of the conversation, but she
could see new manliness and self-reliance in her son.

"Get your mother's bags," Mr. Barnard continued. "Put them in your room. Martha said everything is ready for you to move into the other room."

"What other room?" There was only one other,
and Mrs. Barnard didn't want him there.

"Martha said to be sure to tell you that you are
to have Lewis's room. She has had it all planned for
a long time."

Niki felt a soaring happiness that completely un-
manned him. He had been prepared to defend himself
against Mr. Barnard's displeasure, but his kindness

and Mrs. Barnard's acceptance of him as worthy to occupy the room that had been her son's were entirely unexpected. His voice was husky as he asked, "How could she? We didn't even know for sure that my mother was coming."

"She got it ready in July. The other time you were going to invite her to come." Mr. Barnard laid his hand on Niki's shoulder. "Even if your mother hadn't come, she wanted you to move in there. She's been talking about it for weeks. You certainly know how to get around the ladies. Between Martha and your mother's songs of praise, I expect to see golden wings sprouting from your shoulders almost any day."

"You know how women are," Niki answered with a grin.

It had been quite a day, But tired as he was, Niki laid down his mother's suitcase and went back to Hercules.

"Herky, he likes us! I guess we did all right tonight!"

He held the dog in his arms, vainly trying to escape the caresses of the long red tongue. "Boy, what a wonderful feeling! Everything's going our way!"

Herky wagged what little tail he had because he thought so too. Niki picked up the bag again and went into the house.

Chapter 16 **EVERYBODY HAPPY**

When Niki woke the next morning he lay still, thinking over the events of the busy yesterday. He looked about him at Lewis's room. Lewis's pictures. Lewis's books. The lamp base was a sturdy boatman at his wheel; the bookends were whalemen with poised harpoons. All these things Lewis had loved. And he had loved his father and his mother, and being young, and being alive.

For a long time Niki thought about the mystery of life and death. About his own father, his mother. Of the way she had looked at him last night. Beginning today he would try as he had never tried before to be a good son to her; to keep her happy.

He felt hungry and began to wonder about the time. His watch said twenty minutes of eleven. He looked at it in astonishment. Yes. It was ticking. Gosh! Could he have slept the whole morning? What a thing to do on this day of all days! He bathed and dressed and ran down the stairs in double-quick time. He could hear his mother singing. There she was in the kitchen, as much at home as though she had always lived there, taking a fragrant apple pie out of the Barnard oven.

"Mom, honest, I never did this before," he said as he squeezed oranges and filled a tall glass with the juice.

"We decided not to call you. You had quite a day yesterday."

"You all did," said Niki, pitching into his cereal. "It's grand you could come."

"I wasn't quite sure from that letter whether you wanted me or not, but when I found the Barnards needed me, of course I left everything and came. Weren't you lucky to get a place like this!" She looked around the big kitchen and through the windows to the garden, the fields and hills beyond. "It's like Heaven!"

Niki's eyes followed hers and he saw something

she didn't. The key to the chinchilla house was hanging on the hook beside the window.

"You're right, Mom. It is like Heaven. And if ever there was a pair of saints on earth it's Mr. and Mrs. Barnard."

He did the barn chores and dug potatoes until dinner time.

Immediately after the meal he wanted to show her the chinchillas.

"Come on. Leave the dishes," he teased.

She smiled at him. "No. You go. I'll be along in a few minutes."

He joined Mr. Barnard and helped him repair the door panel, fitting a piece of plywood over the broken place. It was nearly finished when Mrs. Louganis appeared.

"What took you so long?" Niki asked.

"Do you want a full report? I washed the dishes, mopped the kitchen floor, and made your bed."

"You've got a lot to learn. Washing floors is my job, and I take care of my room, too."

Mr. Barnard saw the unbelieving look on her face.

"You — you wash the floors?"

"Sure."

"What about continuing to do it when you get home?" Mr. Barnard asked.

"Mm, I don't know. Do you suppose Granny would faint if she saw me washing her kitchen floor?" Niki laughed, as he got up from his knees beside the door. "Shall I take my mother around now?"

"Go ahead." Charles Barnard took his time fitting the last piece of half-round molding back in place as he listened to the lecture as Niki showed his mother the chinchilla house. Nothing was left out. His mother's interest in what he was saying was surpassed only by her pride in her son.

Niki showed her the twins and told her at great length about his care of them. They came to the wire and nibbled his fingers.

"Do they bite?" she asked.

"Not to be vicious. They bite things like bright buttons out of curiosity. They might nip your fingers a little, but my twins would never bite me."

He seemed unable to get past their cage, but he did not ask to take them out. He fed them cornflakes through the wire so that his mother could see them sit up and use their tiny forepaws.

"Why don't you take them out so she can feel their fur?" Mr. Barnard asked. "And give them their dust pans."

Niki lifted a face radiant with happiness. Very deliberately he winked at Mr. Barnard. "Sure, boss,

I was just going to." Very deliberately, and with great understanding, Mr. Barnard winked back.

"This is a bath pan," Niki explained. " It contains fuller's earth, which is mineral dust, hydrous aluminum silicate. I found that in the dictionary, and when I get to chemistry class I'm going to find out what it means."

Mr. Barnard chuckled appreciatively. Leave it to Niki. He'd like to take the boy to a breeders' convention sometime. He'd make those men sit up and take notice!

"It is a kind of dust that is sometimes used by dry-cleaning establishments," Niki continued. "Chinchillas never bathe in water, but this dust keeps their fur clean. Even the babies know how to use it as soon as they're big enough to climb into the pan."

Mother and son stood together watching Nikita and Mr. Morgan roll and tumble and shake their beautiful coats clean. Niki lifted Nikita out so his mother could feel the shining fur.

"Sure and you're beautiful, so soft and precious," she said. "And does Mr. Morgan know you named one for him?"

"Yes. I wrote to him. I sent him a picture, too."

"Oh, Niki, I thank God it turned out like this." Tears rolled down her face as she looked from the chinchilla to the boy who held it. Quietly Mr. Barnard picked up his tools and left.

It took more than one day to show her everything. She went with Niki to get the cows. She tried her hand at milking.

"I used to do it when we lived on the farm," she said. She loved the gardens, praised the hens, and the good brown eggs.

They walked through the fields where the rowen was ready for mowing. They found a great pine tree with a fresh white scar down the length of it and traced a furrow through the pine needles where the lightning had followed a root and dug a channel into the ground.

"I knew it struck close. I hope I'll never see another storm like that one," Niki said.

"But you like the country, don't you?" she asked, as she picked up handfuls of brown pine needles and crackled them in her fingers.

"Yes, I do. I thought I'd be missing the city but I guess I've been too busy. I hate to leave here. I hate to go back."

"It will be different now. I think things will go all right. Mr. Morgan's going to be pleased about this summer."

"I promised him I wouldn't quit."

"Yes. I remember."

"I'm going to work at school, too. I've made up my mind."

They walked in silence to see the new reservoir. There was no need for words.

The day Mrs. Barnard returned from the hospital was a busy one. Niki and his mother cleaned the house. While she arranged flowers, he washed the porch and the steps, raked the gravel in the drive and clipped the edges of the lawn. No queen ever received a warmer welcome.

The two women liked each other immediately. The family settled into a new routine, satisfactory to all.

Meanwhile, the pump and pipes having arrived, Niki helped Mr. Barnard and Sam set up the irrigating system. The three-inch stationary pipe, costing, Niki learned, three dollars a foot, was laid in the trenches they had dug. Every one hundred feet there was a riser two feet high with outlet and valve to which portable aluminum pipes could be attached. On these were mounted spray nozzles each of which could sprinkle an area a hundred twenty-five feet in diameter, at the rate of thirty gallons a minute.

Niki listened with both ears. It took 27,000 gallons to put one inch of water on an acre, and with pipes the size of theirs it would take two hours sprinkling to do it. That meant a lot of water, especially if Mr. Barnard carried out his intention and went into the nursery business in the fall. But Sam reckoned there were 150,000 gallons of water in the "sump hole," as he called it, and it would take a lot of pumping to run that dry.

After the pipes were laid, a pump with a gasoline engine was installed in a little pumphouse near the pool. A rubber hose twenty feet long with a strainer on the end was dropped into the water. When everything was ready, Niki sprinted up to the house to open the valve on the whirling sprinkler near the screened porch.

"Watch it!" he yelled to his mother and Mrs. Barnard, and raced back to be with the men when they started the engine.

It worked! To Niki it seemed like a miracle as the pump motor chugged away and water began to pour out of the hose attached to the nearest outlet. He dashed back to the house to find the new sprinkler slowly turning to soak the ground and bring back green velvet loveliness to the lawn.

With the irrigating system in, Mr. Barnard began to make plans to convert some of the meadow land to a nursery. For the extra work he would need extra help. Niki hoped he would have the chance to come again next summer. Even if it meant hoeing, he would like to see a nursery of small pines, junipers, and yews.

Everything had worked out so wonderfully this year. And he would have chucked it all away if he had left the night of Mr. Simmons' visit, or if he had gone west with Jokey. Where was Jokey, Niki wondered. Twice he had sent postcards to the old address in care of Mr. Donelly, but no word had come from Jokey.

At the back of Niki's mind there was always one piece of unfinished business. He made inquiries of boys he met at the pond and in town. Nobody knew where Toby was. Various rumors had him joining the Navy, going out on a fishing boat, and working in a drug store, but nobody really knew. Niki had to let it go at that. He wouldn't forget, though. If Mr. Barnard let him work on the ranch next summer, he'd find Toby. Elephants weren't the only ones that remembered!

On Thursday Mr. Barnard said to Niki, "It's time we had a day off. Tomorrow we're going to the city and get you a new outfit for school and we'll go to a ball game. What do you say?"

Niki beamed. "Gosh, I'd love to. Thanks. Thanks a lot."

It was one of the happiest days of Niki's life. They left on an early train, bought the first completely new outfit Niki had ever had — hat, shoes, sweaters, shirts, slacks, a new topcoat, everything. From the store they went to the bank where four fifty-dollar United States Savings Bonds were registered in Niki's name and put for safekeeping in Mr. Barnard's safe deposit box. Next came a steak dinner, followed by an exciting ball game. It was perfect.

Although neither of them mentioned it, that day marked a milestone in their lives. It was the end of Niki's trial period, the beginning of a friendship that had been earned. Niki realized for the first time that after he left for Warren Mr. Barnard was going to miss him as much as he would miss Mr. Barnard. And that was a lot. It was a day neither of them would ever forget.

Chapter 17 **THE WINNER**

Labor Day weekend. Only Saturday, Sunday, Monday left. Niki wished he could hold back the days. The sparkling mornings with a touch of frost in the air, the bright warm afternoons, the cozy evenings by the open fire. Why did they have to slip by so fast!

Saturday and Sunday they took short rides through the back roads to show his mother some pretty places. Mrs. Barnard was improving every day, so she went, too. Then Saturday was gone, and Sunday, and only Monday left.

"Is there anything special you'd like to do tomorrow?" Mr. Barnard asked.

"I'd like to go to the swimming meet at Robbins Pond pavilion. It begins at two o'clock."

"Do you want to go in the races?"

"No, I can't do that because I didn't sign up, but a lot of kids that I know will be there."

"All right. We'll go."

It turned out to be the best of those never-to-be-forgotten days that can highlight a summer.

As soon as his chores were done, Niki went for one last swim at Indian Pond. There were already many people there.

"How much longer are you staying, Niki?" the boys asked.

"Going back tomorrow."

"See you next summer."

"I hope." Mr. Barnard still had not mentioned next summer. Niki wondered why. Perhaps he was getting a man to help right through the year. Maybe he didn't want to make commitments so far in advance. But whatever the reason for his silence, Niki couldn't help hoping.

When he returned to the house there was a ritzy green Ford, a four-door hardtop sedan, parked in the drive. He had never seen that car in Bristol. He walked around to look at the number plates. New York!

The living room was full of people. By the abruptness with which the conversation stopped, Niki knew they had been talking about him. His face flushed with pleasure when he saw who it was.

"Mr. Morgan!" he grabbed the outstretched hand, his eyes glowing with excitement. "This is great! I never expected to see you here, but am I glad you could come!"

"It's certainly nice to see you, Niki," Mr. Morgan answered. He turned to the lady by his side. "Frances, this is Niki Louganis. Niki, Mrs. Morgan."

"I've heard so much about you, Niki," she said, "and you look just as I expected you would."

Niki made a swipe at his damp hair and everybody laughed.

"We're on our way from Maine, so we detoured to include Bristol. I want to see my namesake," said Mr. Morgan.

"Sure. I'm proud to show him. Can you come now?"

"I'd be glad to."

"Let's go with them, Frances," Mr. Barnard whispered. "This will be worth hearing."

While his mother and Mrs. Barnard made sand-

wiches for lunch, Niki escorted the rest of the party
to the chinchilla house. With no detail omitted, he
explained to an appreciative audience the intricacies
of chinchilla care. The old confident swagger was
there, but the thought that this was the last time
Nikita would sit on his shoulder and nibble his ear
gave an earnestness to his words.

"You're very fond of them, aren't you?" Mr.
Morgan asked as he followed Niki from cage to cage.

"I sure am. I'll miss them all right." He sighed
as he looked around the building. The bright look
of animation left his face. "Yes, I'll certainly miss
them."

As they left the chinchilla house, Mr. Morgan
asked, "What do you hear from Jokey?"

"He's been here. He's got a car, a slick job. He
built it himself. He wanted me to go to Denver with
him because his father's there."

"Yes. He told me about it."

"He did?" Niki looked up in surprise. "When
did you see him?"

"Well, you see, he started for Denver. Mr. Donelly notified me, of course, and the State Police
found him for us. He got as far as Indiana. I think
he was glad to be picked up because his money was
all gone and he hadn't had anything to eat for a
couple of days."

Niki shook his head. "That's tough. I wish he could have got to his father's."

Mr. Morgan smiled. "He did get there. He finally persuaded me to go to Denver with him."

"You're kidding!"

"No, I'm not kidding. I wanted to see his father, and I wanted to know Jokey better. The boy's all right, but he was in real trouble right then."

"He was? What happened?" Niki looked up anxiously.

"Well, a boy can't lie about his age and use another fellow's birth certificate without getting found out sooner or later. This business will be on file at the Registry office. It could have landed him in Juvenile Court. As it is, he'll find that when he gets to be sixteen the Registry will be in no hurry to give him a license no matter how well he can drive."

"Gee, I was afraid he'd get into trouble. That fellow in the garage didn't help him much."

"Arthur Perry? No. He's in trouble up to his neck because the car was registered to him and driven by an unlicensed, under-aged operator with his knowledge and consent. He'll probably lose his job and his license, too. You know all these State Police and Registry officers have teletype hookup. It doesn't take them long to get word back to the state where a car is registered."

"I hadn't thought of that."

"Jokey hadn't, either. If I hadn't gone out there and worked on this case for days, explaining just what the situation was and making dozens of phone calls, Jokey would be in reform school now. If he'd had an accident there wouldn't have been a thing in the world anybody could have done to help him."

"What became of the car?" Niki remembered how the motor had purred.

"It's registered to his father. He seems to be a fine man. He has a nice wife and a nice home. I can see no reason why everything shouldn't work out well. He has a good job in a big garage, and Jokey's a born mechanic. It looks like a good set-up, and the boy is where he belongs."

"Anybody who could fix up an old heap and make it run like his car did really has the know-how. I hope he'll get a license before very long." Wasn't it funny how things worked out, Niki thought. If he had gone with Jokey it wouldn't have helped. With two of them to get hungry the money wouldn't have lasted as long as it did. And Jokey was all right now. Niki looked at Mr. Morgan with new appreciation. What a friend he was, going way out to Denver to help one of his boys!

"I'm glad he can live with his father," Niki said at last.

"So am I. And I'm glad you worked out of your own troubles. I'm glad Charles Barnard gave you that last chance."

"Some day I'll repay him for the loss of Hooper."

"You must. It's something to work for, and I know you can accomplish anything you set your heart on. You've got it in you. I've always known it."

"But I can't repay him for a lot of other things."

Mr. Morgan thumped Niki on the back. "He's made a man of you, Niki."

Overhearing the remark, Charles Barnard smiled. "While compliments are flying, I want to say for Niki that he earned his way this summer. I've had several boys work for me at one time or another, but never one that worked so faithfully. Come on, now. Let's get something to eat. Then we'll all go to the swimming races."

Since this was a special occasion, Niki dressed up. He chose a light blue sport shirt and put on his new slacks. He pinched the wave back into his damp hair and surveyed himself in the mirror, pleased with what he saw. June would surely be in the races. He hoped to talk to her. He adjusted his collar, straightened his new tie, squared his shoulders and grinned at his reflection. Yes, sir! He certainly hoped to meet June this afternoon.

They arrived early at the pond and parked the car so that Mrs. Barnard could see the races without having to stand up so long. The crowd was already gathering.

"Wouldn't you like some ice cream?" Niki asked. He wanted to do something for his friends. "I'll get us some cones."

"Can you carry six?" his mother asked.

"Sure, Mom, and I'll remember the paper napkins, too, a big bunch of them. I'll carry the cones this way." He spread his fingers wide apart and she laughed. She was worrying about his new clothes, he knew.

The ice cream stand was doing a big business. As Niki took his place in line he kept hoping he would see June or Joe in the crowd. It was hard to realize that by this time tomorrow he would be on his way back to the city. He looked across the pond to the tall pines that hid the Simmons' camp, remembering the night he and Joe had slept out under the stars. Some difference from the daybed in Grandmother Przybyzewski's living room!

The man at the window handed him his cones, and with three in each hand, and a bunch of paper napkins under his arm, he made his way toward the car.

"Niki! Oh, Niki!"

He turned and saw June running toward him.
"Oh, Niki," she panted, "I was hoping you would
come."

"I was hoping, too," he said.

"Don't you look nice all dressed up!"

"So do you. You always look nice." She wore
the same yellow bathing suit she had worn the first
time he saw her. He stood still, rooted to the spot
beside her, wanting never to leave it. "You always
look nice," he repeated.

An impish dimple showed in her cheek. "Like the
moonlight?" she asked. "Do you remember you
said that once, that I was like the moonlight? I
never forgot it, for it's the nicest thing anybody ever
said to me."

"No, not like the moonlight in the middle of the
afternoon," he said with a grin. "Like a—a butterfly." He gave a slow, appraising glance that started
with her hair and slid down to her sun-browned feet.
"Like a big brown and yellow butterfly. How do you
like that?"

"Oh, Niki," she giggled, tossing her hair back
over her shoulders, "you're awfully funny, the things
you say."

"Funny? What's funny about that?" he asked,
falling in step beside her as she walked towards the
beach. "Which races are you in?"

"Only the 100 yards. I hope I'll win the prize. I was on the committee that chose them." She pulled her hair back and twisted it into a tight knot, ducked her head and pulled on the yellow swim cap while Niki marveled at the complete disappearance of the fluffy gold. As she fastened the chin-strap she added, "I suppose you've heard about Toby."

"No. What about him?" Niki asked, scowling. That piece of unfinished business still rankled, and he hated to leave Bristol without giving the big bully the punishment he deserved.

"He's gone. Joined the Navy, and am I glad!"

"Oh." Niki's face fell when he heard the words. "Well, that does it I guess," he said slowly, "but sometime I'm going to —"

"Forget it, Niki," June interrupted. "Look, they're lining up. I've got to go," she said. "I'll see you after the races."

"Wait, June. I haven't told you anything yet. My mother's here and Mr. Morgan and I want you to meet them and —"

"Afterwards, Niki. And look out for that ice cream."

"Yuh. Guess I'd better." For some time he had been conscious that the piled-high cones were growing soft and that a gooey stickiness was gradually coating his fingers and traveling towards his wrists.

At that moment it had reached a stage of drippiness that, once June was gone, became something to be concerned about. He couldn't shift the cones, he couldn't reach the napkins. The only solution seemed to be to dump the whole business in the trash can and start over again.

He looked up to see June's father watching him.

"Need some help?" he asked.

"I guess I do," Niki replied, hardly able to believe that Mr. Simmons would be willing to help. Together they wiped up the overflow and wrapped each cone in a couple of napkins. Mr. Simmons held them while Niki washed his hands at the drinking fountain.

"Thanks," Niki said, taking his cones again, and wondering what miracle had brought about the change.

"I was looking for June."

"She was here a minute ago."

"Yes, I know." Mr. Simmons chewed his lip and looked at Niki. "She wants me to talk to Mr. Barnard. My wife does, too."

Niki studied the man's face, trying to figure out what was coming. It was something pretty important, judging by the deep wrinkles in his forehead.

"They've always thought you were on the level, and I guess they're right."

"Thanks for saying that. I'm trying to be. Honest, I am. I wish you'd come with me now and see Mr. Barnard, and meet my mother, and Mr. Morgan, the principal of my school."

"All right."

They were soon there, and the ice cream distributed. The introductions and explanations that followed were interrupted by the boom of the starting gun, and the swimming races were on. Mrs. Morgan stayed in the car with Mrs. Barnard while the others joined the crowd near the wharf.

Niki moved forward with his mother to watch the younger children's races, and to point out June and Joe if he could find them among the waiting contestants. When he turned back, he saw the three men talking together and heard Mr. Simmons say, "And when you gave him another chance, I knew you must believe in him." And Mr. Barnard's reply, "He promised me—"

Niki moved farther away, with a quick, hurting tightness in the back of his throat as he remembered the morning he had said it. He watched the next relay race without speaking, busy with his thoughts.

Then the starter brought him out of it, announcing over the loud speaker, "Fifteen—sixteen-year-old girls' class. Ready for the 100-yard race!"

Hearing it, the men crowded close beside them.

"June!" Niki yelled, "Hi, June!" and as she turned to look up, he threw one arm around Mr. Barnard's neck and the other around her father's.

She stared in amazement at the three smiling faces.

"We want a winner! We want a winner," they shouted together.

And then the swimmers were off, down the pond, circling a red skiff that had been moored as a turning point, racing back again to the cheering crowd on shore. The yellow cap came in first, and a silver flying fish was pinned on the yellow bathing suit.

In another minute June was with them. "I had to win," she announced. "I couldn't wait another minute to find out what's going on here." She slipped her hand into her father's and glanced quickly around the circle of faces.

"June, I want you to meet my mother," Niki said proudly.

Quickly June unpinned her flying fish and fastened it at the neck of Mrs. Louganis' dress. "You wear it," she said impulsively. "You have a winner in your family, too."

"I have?" Niki's mother was finding it hard to keep up with the surprises of this unusual day.

"Mm," June answered, smiling at her and then at Niki and making his ears turn pink. "And next summer you'll race, won't you, Niki!"

"You bet I will," he answered, and then wished he hadn't, for Mr. Barnard gave him a queer, surprised look and said nothing. He probably thinks I've got a nerve, expecting to come again, Niki thought.

Again the introductions were interrupted by the starter's announcement. The fifteen—sixteen-year-old boys' race was about to begin.

"Come on," Niki said, and he and June pushed their way through the crowd to watch Joe. He was easy to find, his red head gleaming in the sun near the lead, pulling ahead on the last stretch and, with a final spurt of speed, winning by a length. Niki yelled himself hoarse, cheering Joe on.

Hardly waiting for him to receive his award, a silver belt buckle, Niki and June dragged him away to meet the others. As it was time for the Morgans to be on their way, the older people soon returned to the car, but Niki waited for the Simmonses to set off in Joe's catboat for camp. Again and again they said the same old farewells that can mean so little, or so much.

Good old Joe! What a pal he was! A true friend. And June . . . Niki sighed.

Well, it was over. Tomorrow at this time he would be home again. Back in the city with Granny. And then school. It had been good here, but it was over, and the real test lay ahead. He walked slowly back to Mr. Morgan's car.

Again he sensed that they had been talking about him. His mother's face was flushed and her eyes were dancing. Well, that was something. It must be good things they were saying.

"Niki," Mr. Barnard began, "we've been having a conference — Mr. Morgan, your mother, Martha, all of us. How would you like to make Bristol your permanent home? Your mother will stay on as our housekeeper, if you are sure you would be happy here."

Niki looked from him to his mother, letting the wonderful words sink in.

"Stay here?" he repeated. "Live here all the time? How could we? What would Granny do?"

"I think Aunt Katie would be glad to live with her."

"Oh, Mr. Barnard!" Niki's voice ended in a squeak. No more words came, but none were needed.

"Make it Uncle Charlie."

But Niki was flying towards the wharf waving both arms and yelling, "*June! Joe! Listen!*"

The words floated over the still water. The people in the car waited for the answering shout.

"What is it?"

"*See you Wednesday!*"

"What did you say?"

"*I said see you Wednesday. At the new high school. I'm going to live here all the time with Uncle Charlie Barnard. I'm not going back to Warren!*"

"Whoops!" came the answer, and first June and then Joe was overboard, racing back toward the wharf where Niki, his arms waving like a human windmill, whooped back at them.

And Mr. Simmons, realizing that he had an interest in all that was happening, slowly took the tiller and turned the boat around.

That Niki was quite a boy!

Wisconsin State College at Eau Claire
LIBRARY RULES

No book should be taken from the library until it has been properly charged by the librarian.

Books may be kept one week but are not to be renewed without special permission of the librarian.

A fine of two cents a day will be charged for books kept over time.

In case of loss or injury the person borrowing this book will be held responsible for a part or the whole of the value of a new book.

DUE	DUE	DUE	DUE
Jan 10 '58	Jan 7 '59	Jul 25 '61	MAR 19 '70
Jan 21 '58	Jan 22 '59	Oct 9	
Jan 29 '58	Feb 27 '59	Oct 10	
Feb 14 '58	Sep 28 '59	Apr 23	
Mar 12 '58	Nov 12 '59	May 14	
Mar 14 '58	Jan 12 '60	May 21	
Apr 22 '58	Jan 19 '60	May 22	
May 1 '58	Ap 25 '60	Oct 23 62	
May 15 '58	Oct 13 '60	Nov 1 62	
May 23 '58	Oct 20 '60	Jan 7 63	
Sep 23 '58	Nov 17 '60	Dec 20 63	
Oct 1 '58	Dec 8 '60	Jan 12	
Oct 14 '58	Jan 5 '61	NOV 12 '65	
Oct 31 '58		FEB 28 '67	
Oct 31 '58		MAR 7 '67	
Nov 7 '58		MAR 23 '67	
		OCT 16	